CW01509414

CAGES AND C

Andrew Michael Hurley

Lime Tree Press
England
www.geocities.com/limetreepress/home

CAGES AND OTHER STORIES

Copyright © 2006 Andrew Michael Hurley.

All Rights Reserved

No part of this book may be reproduced in any form, by photocopying or by any electronic or mechanical means, including information storage or retrieval systems, without permission in writing from both the copyright holder and the publisher of this book.

ISBN 978 1 4116 9902 1

First published 2006 by

Lime Tree Press
England
www.geocities.com/limetreepress/home

Printed in Great Britain for Lime Tree Press

CAGES AND OTHER STORIES

Acknowledgments

Cages was first published in *Libbon* Magazine and *Muse* Magazine in 2005; *Tell Me Again About the Thunder* and *The Cuckoo and the Magpie* were first published in *Transmission* magazine in 2005; *When I brought you back to the North Country* first appeared in *Transmission* magazine in 2006

For Jo, Ben, Tom and the memory of Robert Platt.

Andrew Michael Hurley was born in 1975 and has lived in Manchester and London. He now lives in Lancashire where he teaches English literature. This is his first collection of short stories.

Cage *n.* An enclosure of twigs or wire in which birds are kept; a place for wild beasts; a prison for petty malefactors

Webster's Dictionary 1857

The Cuckoo & the Magpie

Even in the afternoon the room was still dark, so she tugged the cord of each long blind and they shot up, one by one, allowing sunlight to enter, shaped into rectangles by the dust her movements had stirred. She tried the windows and opened two of them; the third was painted shut and, after scratching away some of the paint from the frame with her nails, her face became downcast.

Yet, with the room exposed to light she was able to convince herself that she could remember it as it was when they had first moved there some twenty years earlier; a large, high-ceilinged square with a fireplace opposite the windows and walls full of dark shapes where paintings had been.

At the far end of the room was a door that would not open and she had waited for the landlord to bring the key. When it arrived it was anonymous amongst the heavy bunch that he posted through the letterbox.

Her husband entered, carrying a box of ornaments and books under one arm and in the other hand he held a birdcage.
'Put him over by the window, so he can get some air,' she said and he did so, struggling not to drop all the things he held. The bird peeped and chattered and he tapped on the bars, making kissing noises.
'He's just like the old one, isn't he?' she said. 'Just like Marcel.'
'He wasn't called Marcel,' he replied. 'And anyway, it was a she last time.'
'It wasn't. It was a boy and we called him Marcel.'
'As in Proust?'
'As in Marceau,' she replied. 'He used to copy me all the time."
'Did he?'
'He was always at it. He used to nod his head if I did, or walk around in circles, or sing.'

11

'Marcel Marceau didn't sing,' he teased her.
'Don't be facetious,' she said. 'You know what I mean.'

'Why don't we call this one Marcel, if it makes you happy?' he suggested and she seemed pleased.
'This is exactly how we started last time,' she smiled. 'Do you remember? We drove here in that tiny little car with Marcel in the passenger seat. He was the first thing we brought into this room. And here we are again.'

They both became silent for a moment and watched the bird, a canary, pecking at a dangling block of seed.

'If we can do everything as we did it before it'll be like a second chance,' she said, following the bird's movements.

The canary hopped onto a swing, making a little bell tinkle and nuzzled its wings with its beak.

'Do you remember what colour we painted the woodwork in here?' she asked. 'I was trying to find it underneath the white.'
'It was green, I think. Or yellow,' he said. 'I can't remember.'
'Yes, it was yellow, I think, like Marcel. We painted it the same colour as him didn't we?'

'If you say so.'

He set the box of ornaments down and went over to the nearest window. Making a visor with his hand, he looked down into the street.

'I'd forgotten how busy London was,' he said.
'It was never that busy around *here*,' she replied. 'It was always rather deserted.'

'Do you remember that tree out there?' he said and she came over to the window.
'Oh, yes, don't you? It was always full of magpies.'

'I don't remember that.'

'You do. There was that nest. Full of coins and necklaces.'

'Are you sure it's always been there?' He looked doubtful

'Look how tall it is,' she said. 'It's hundreds of years old.'

'But we used to be able to see the river from here.'

'Don't be silly,' she laughed. 'The river's miles away. We used to have to cycle there.'

'But we used to sit and watch the boats. We used to play that game about where each one was going.'

'Not from here,' she fanned herself with her hands.

'Do you remember the one with the rainbow coloured sail that sank?'

'I think so,' she yawned.

'It used to come along every week and then one day it tipped over,' he looked out of the window again, trying to see the river through the branches. 'You must remember that. The mast cracked and floated away with all those people hanging on to it.'

She shook her head and walked over to the fireplace, running her fingers over the mantelpiece. He wiped sweat away from his brow and picked at the flaking paintwork, chipping fragments away from the wall which landed amongst the dried rose petals in the corner of the window.

'Are you glad we came back?' she said looking at her blackened fingertips.

'I don't know yet.'

'God it's hot,' she sighed and went back over to the jammed window at the far end of the room, struggling with it once more. He came to help and between them they slid it upwards making the sound of traffic more insistent.

Out of the window they could see the queue of cars waiting to get onto a roundabout at the top of the street, which led to other London suburbs, then others.

'I still think it's wonderful that we got our old place back,' she said. He nodded and wiped his forehead again.

'I know you weren't keen at first about coming back but this is where we belong,' she moved closer to him. 'This is where we're good together.'

'I'm sure we used to be able to see the river from here,' he said.

'It'll be like starting again,' she tried to regain eye contact with him but he was looking at the keys in her hand.

'Any luck?' he asked.

She sighed. 'I've not tried them yet. They came while you were out. I'll see if they work.'

One by one she rattled keys in the lock and then accidentally dropped the bunch, forgetting which ones she had already tried.

'What's in there, anyway?' he asked

'The safe,' she replied and began a system of trying a key and removing it from the enormous steel ring if it did not work.

'What safe?'

'The safe in the wall behind the picture of the boat.'

'Oh, that old thing,' he said. 'There's nothing in it, is there?'

'I put something in it before we left,' she threw another key into the growing pile.

The bird clattered in the cage and they both turned their heads towards it.

'Do you remember when we bought Marcel?' she said, returning her attention to the door

'This one or the other one?'

'The old one,' she said and using both hands tried to twist a long black key.

'I bought it from the old man who lived downstairs,' he said.

'We bought it together, in that shop in Chiswick,' she said the last word through gritted teeth and gave up with the key and discarded it.

'It was the old man's,' he insisted. 'Don't you remember him? He lived on the ground floor. Huge beard. Always wore his medals.'

'Mrs Eddrington lived on the ground floor,' she said. 'I don't remember any old man.'

'Maybe it was her husband.'

'No, she was a widow. Her husband died in Normandy. She used to tell us every time we saw her.'

'No, that was the old man. He *fought* at Normandy.'

'Oh, it doesn't matter,' she snapped. 'Why will none of these keys work?'

He shrugged and began to pace slowly, scuffing at the dust with his feet.

She cursed under her breath and then the last key slid into the lock with a smoothness that set it apart from the others. She looked over at him and smiled, but the key would not revolve. In frustration, she twisted it too hard and let out a yelp when her hand slipped and the key gashed her skin.

She went over to the window, wiping blood on her jeans and then sucking the edge of her palm.

'Are you alright?' he asked. She moved her head and rubbed the knuckle of her thumb against her eyes.

'Have you seen what they've done to the fireplace,' she said, staring outside.

'It was always like that, wasn't it?'

'What, all boarded up?' she turned, frowning. 'No, it had all those beautiful tiles around the edges.'

'But we never *used* it, did we?'

'Of course we used it. Don't you remember all those nights in the winter when we had no money and you'd sit and read by the fire and I'd play cards or something?'

'Cards?'

'Yes, cards, you know, patience or something like that.'

'You never play cards.'

'Perhaps I could start again,' she said. 'Open it up, will you? I want to see it.'

He went over to the boxes that had been dumped in the corner of the room and after rummaging in one and then another he found a long screwdriver, which he used to lever the board away enough for him to get his hands behind it. Looking along the top edge of the wood, he placed his fingers in between the nails that had been exposed and pulled at the board, ripping it off in three tugs.

The fireplace was bare brick and crumbling mortar, the cavity dressed with cobwebs that moved in the air blowing down the chimney.

On the floor, behind the grate, a magpie lay dead in a sludge of ashes, dust and rain. One of its wings was missing and its eyes had gone white and leaked. He turned it over with the end of the screwdriver and its remaining wing flopped to one side exposing its belly where the ribcage pressed through mutton coloured flesh that was stripped of feathers. A piece of red meat hung out of its open beak.

'You might be right about that tree,' he said and she came over.
'It must have fallen down the chimney, poor thing,' she said.
'Does that happen?'
'I should think so. God, what's it been eating?' she noticed the pulpy mass in its mouth.
'I think that's its heart,' he said and she backed away.

'It's like that story isn't it?' she said quietly.
'What story?'
'*The Cuckoo and the Magpie*. Don't you know it?' he shook his head.
'It's about the cuckoo that tries to find a nest to lay her egg in and she flies around and around but can't find one anywhere.'
'It sounds familiar,' he said. 'Doesn't the cuckoo die or something?'
'No, not the cuckoo,' she said. 'It's the magpie that dies.'
'Go on.'
'Well, eventually the cuckoo sees a nest on top of a chimney and finds that there are three eggs in it already. So she takes one out and lays hers there instead. Anyway, the nest belongs to a magpie that comes back and carries on warming the eggs, not realising that one of them belongs to the cuckoo.'

16

She began to take out ornaments from the box as she spoke and arrange them on the mantelpiece. One came out in two pieces, a small stone chameleon, whose head fell with a thump onto the floor.

'I thought that might break,' she said. 'It's been fixed that many times.'

'Do you want me to glue it again?'

'Do you think it'll work?'

He nodded and she bent to pick up the chameleon's head and gave the two pieces to him.

'So, what happens to the magpie then?'

'Oh, it's really not that interesting,' she said dismissively.

'Come on.'

'Well, the cuckoo's egg grows quicker than the others and it's so beautiful that the magpie steals jewellery and coins and precious stones and things to decorate the nest. But the gifts get so heavy that the other eggs crack and the chicks die, but the magpie only cares about the beautiful egg and waits and waits for it to hatch, trying to stay awake so that she doesn't miss it. But, of course she falls asleep and the cuckoo hatches and pushes the magpie down the chimney.'

He smiled. 'And the moral is?'

She smiled back sarcastically and blew the dust off a porcelain figurine. 'I always wondered what happened to the egg the cuckoo took away.'

'I think they just throw them out of the nest,' he replied and leant the board against the fireplace.

'I suppose they must,' she said. 'But it just seemed to disappear.'

The canary twittered and the mirror in its cage reflected a bright circle that moved across the walls.

'Shall I give it some water?' he asked.

She nodded and he went to the kitchen, returning with a plastic jug of water.

17

They went over to the bird and he gave her the jug to hold while he opened the cage. The bird fluttered and scuffled as he reached in to take its bowl, then suddenly flew at the open doorway. He tried to trap it with his arm but he was afraid of hurting it and let it go.

She shrieked as the bird flashed past her face and swung upwards into the corner of the room where it perched on the picture rail. The water jug hit the floor and spread a dark stain across the bare wood. The bird dove into the room and circled twice before going back to its place in the corner. She closed the windows quickly and stood with her back to the room.

'I can't look at it,' she said quietly.

He made clucking noises and the bird looked at him before swooping down again. She screamed as it fluttered close to the back of her head. He took the seed block out of the cage and dangled it in front of him and then put it on the floor. The bird came down again and he tried to catch it but missed.

'We'll never catch it,' he said.
'Make it come down!' she yelled.
'Isn't this what happened to the first one?'
'It flew away,' she sobbed. 'It got out of the window.'
'Well, We'll just have to wait.'
'Don't let it near me,' she said. 'I can't stand its wings in my face.'

She became very still and when he looked at her, out of the window, he saw that the tree was gone and a boat was turning on its side in the river, its rainbow coloured sail drifting away.

He opened his mouth to speak but the bird distracted him as it came down and began to eat the seed. Edging closer he held his hand steadily next to it and then grabbed the bird in his fist. A wing got loose and it tried to fly away again, its yellow feathers patting the air and its head tipped back as if it were trying not to drown. It struggled and pecked at his skin but he held it firm and went back to the cage.

Turning the bird sideways, he tried to thrust his whole hand in but caught the bird's head between the bars and broke its neck.

There was a sound behind him. He turned and saw that she was lying on the floor underneath the window.

As he lifted her he felt her body cracking and saw fracture lines forming over her skin. He put her down and she seemed to flake. Tiny irregular shapes came away from her and then, as he put his fingers to her arms, larger fragments, like pieces of a smashed light bulb, fell onto the floor.

He touched her face and it broke off in his hands. Her hair crackled as he held the back of her head, as though he was crushing a sheaf of dead twigs. Her clothes sagged and became flat.

He tried to embrace her but her body became a scattering of eggshell on the floor.

The pilot of the leaden marshes

And we forget because we must – not because we will
Matthew Arnold, *Absence*

In the morning Jasmine left the hotel early to go to her conference. I stayed in bed for a while longer, listening to the rush of traffic and sirens through the open windows, aware of the enormity of the city that lay outside. I got up and made coffee and looked at the river through the window. The water was slow and wide and I watched a man hauling a rowing boat out of a mud bank on the other side. A dog bounded around his legs. Eventually the man edged the nose of the boat into the water and the dog leapt aboard and the man followed it, digging the end of an oar into the sludge and pushing them afloat. A barge went past and the man and the dog rose and fell on the wake.

I went down to breakfast and had more coffee and read a newspaper and then went back to the room, still feeling tired, wanting to crawl back into bed and forget the museum.

Jasmine's underwear was still on the bed and I thought about the night before when it had been too hot to sleep and she'd stayed up late with her book. She was trying to learn French verbs but got bored by all the changes that had to be memorised and instead learnt to say everything in the present tense and end the sentence with either *yesterday* or *tomorrow*. She made me laugh.

I switched on the television while I brushed my teeth. It was the news. Smoke rising behind palm trees. Concrete buildings shattered. Roofs collapsed. Then men and women in robes wailing near a crater, searching with their hands. Soldiers standing on top of rubble shouting. Feet protruding from under white sheets. Ambulances.

There were policemen outside the Tube station watching the crowds, one of them filming the entranceway with a camera; the others were holding machine guns. They had a dog with them, which occasionally lurched towards people that passed by. I bought a ticket and waited for the train. It was breathless down there and a warm wind blew along the tunnel.

On the train a woman passed along the carriages selling copies of the *Socialist Worker*. No one looked at her. I was standing by the door and she stood opposite me, waiting to get off. I looked at the cover of the paper: a dismembered child covered in rags and blood being held aloft by its distraught mother – *This is what imperialism looks like.*

When I got to the museum it was already busy. People were strewn about on the grass outside, or on the steps. A group of children were being shown around a Panzer by a man in a grey German uniform. Others took photographs of the sculptures in the grounds: a Henry Moore and some other abstract things.

Inside the entrance hall it was cool and still and the marble floor made echoes that rose upwards into the domed ceiling. I walked quickly across to the reception desk, stupidly feeling guilty about Mr Feeney.

Although he insisted in his letters that I should ask for him if I ever visited the museum, I had decided not to tell Mr Feeney that I was there. I didn't want any fuss. My father wouldn't have wanted a fuss either. I felt slightly uneasy about giving the photographs and whatnot to Mr Feeney anyway. They were private to my father. And every time I had sent off an envelope full of stuff to Mr Feeney I felt as if I was betraying him in some way.

I had tried to do something with them. We'd all been overwhelmed when we found boxes full of photographs and letters in the attic after my father had died. I had a spurt of organising them but I never seemed to have time to do it properly. Jasmine suggested the museum. I put it off for a while but the photographs started to loom in the house. Jasmine didn't like seeing them. They seemed too large for me to keep somehow.

Jasmine said it was better that they were preserved properly and put on display.

But it felt like I was passing on a problem.

The last letter from Mr Feeney came a week before we went to London. The exhibition was ready.

A woman at the reception desk pointed me towards the first floor and I began to think about when my father told me the story of the rat and gave me the star and the swastika.

It was evening time on Christmas Day and my father was drunk on gin. My mother was asleep upstairs. I asked him about the camp.

'I'll tell you,' he said, 'but you don't tell anyone else, understand?'

He told me that when the rest of the Red Army arrived at the gates of Auschwitz, he was ten miles behind digging his jeep out of a snowdrift. There were two others with him, boys barely out of school who worked like machines, flinging the snow from the ditch over the wall into the field next to the road. One of them felt his spade bite into something solid and as they continued to dig they uncovered the bodies of a man and woman, bloated and frozen. All three of them stood looking at the bodies and then my father got into the jeep and started the engine. The two boys put their hands against the back of the vehicle, their arms stretched awkwardly over the corpses and skidded and slipped as my father revved the accelerator.

'It's no use,' one of them said. The two boys stepped up onto the bodies and pushed again, this time enabling the jeep to grip the edge of solid concrete and eventually pull itself onto the road.

They arrived at the camp half an hour later, finding black smoke billowing out of buildings. They walked through the brick archway along the railway tracks and found Babel on the unloading platform.

He was shouting to another soldier who was directing prisoners past the camera, "the children first!" The soldier put his hand up to stop a line of stripe-suited men and they dutifully waited while a group of children wandered diffidently over to an official who was taking their names. Babel put his eye back to the viewfinder and held the camera steady as the children walked past. My father got out his camera and took some photographs of Babel and of the children and the men waiting by the gate.

When the children had passed, Babel waved to the soldier and the men were allowed to go. Babel saw my father and helped him up onto the platform.

'It is so cold here,' he said. 'We are all cold. Have a cigarette.'

My father took one and Babel led him through into the camp. They could say nothing to each other.

They went into one of the sleeping quarters and found bodies in the wooden stalls that were once stables and still had the iron rings for tying horses attached to them. They passed a row of people standing behind an electric fence. Some were wrapped in blankets and apart from the sunken eyes looked unharmed, yet when they adjusted the blankets to cover themselves more closely they saw that they were no more than bones smeared with a jaundiced wax. They found a girl wandering alone with a violin in her hand. Three men cooking something in a pot over a fire. Women crying.

Near the officers' mess they saw a number of bodies. Some had heads missing, some were pulp. My father found a German overcoat on the floor and took the swastika armband from it. A group of prisoners were standing around a bonfire on which reams of paper were burning. Some of the prisoners were trying to retrieve the papers with sticks but could not reach them or tipped them further into the fire. No one spoke. A swastika flag was brought out of a building by two other prisoners and between them they laid it over the fire where it ballooned, then curled and shrivelled and expired with the paper, the heat blowing large black flakes into the sky. My father caught one of these flakes and it instantly turned into ash in his palm.

As they went back to the entrance they came across a vast barracks room full of clothes, mounds of brown and black fabric, covering the floor entirely and hanging from crossbeams and rafters. My father bent down and picked up a suit jacket, which apart from the dust looked brand new. On the breast a yellow star hung limply forward and my father plucked it off and showed it to Babel.

Babel turned it over in his hands and picked off the stray threads and gave it back to my father. Then they stayed and looked at the room full of clothes and other stars that were visible.

That Christmas, drunk on the cheap gin that smelled like diesel on his breath, my father gave the star and the swastika to me and I kept them in a box under my bed.

I used to beg him to show me the photographs he had taken at the camp and he would pretend that most of them were lost. The ones that I did see were devoid of people; they were of buildings and fences and fields. He would hand me a wad of black and white photographs and drink gin while I went through them and asked questions that he answered evasively. I remember looking at shot after shot of burning buildings, twisted metal, shattered brick and ruins; but there were others too: a shot of one of the gas chambers that looked like the subway under the bus station: a train wagon that, according to my father, was literally stuffed full of bodies: a mound of striped prayer shawls: sacks of hair.

There were several photographs of the electric fence, its length and height recorded in my father's small, neat handwriting on the back. There was a picture of one of the corner posts of the fence, studded with the black spheres of insulators from which wires radiated for hundreds of yards; and with the post's curved top the whole thing looked like a Cubist harp.

In all there must have been a hundred photographs but there was one that I would always look at last, and savour ghoulishly, the one of the rat, stiff-looking with sweaty fur, lying in its blood on a tiled floor.

And that Christmas he told me what had happened.

He looked at me for a moment, before hoisting himself up out of the chair and going over to the bookcase beside the fire. He prodded at the spines of the books, turning his head to read them until he located the one he wanted and pulled it out. It was not a book but a box and in it was his pistol. He took it out and gave it to me. It felt cold in my hand and it hurt my wrist to hold it. I looked at it more closely and thought that it smelled of old coins.

'Look,' he said, 'here's where the bullets go.' And he slid out a magazine from the handle. 'Snap it back in.' I feebly moved the magazine upwards with my palm but it slid out again and my father smiled and smacked it back into the handle with a force that scared me.

'Babel found the rat,' he said and put the pistol back in the box. 'We were searching some of the buildings and we found a room where there were women lying under sheets.'

He poured more gin and I listened to the clock ticking on the mantelpiece while he thought about what to say next. I looked at the Christmas tree lights and the porcelain figures in the nativity scene arranged on a low table next to the fire. He coughed and started wheezing and I thought about how tired he looked, how he sagged in that chair.

'Babel tried to find out who the women were,' he continued, 'but there was nothing, so we wrote down their height, what we thought their age was, anything. But there was something strange about the last woman we came to; her stomach was moving.'

He drained his glass and put it down on the table next to his armchair.

'Babel looked at me and then turned back to the woman and the rat came out from between the woman's legs. Babel fainted and I shot it.'

He did not look at me.

'What was it doing inside the lady?' I asked.
'It was living inside her womb,' my father said, still not looking at me. 'Do you know what a womb is?' He must have seen me nodding because he nodded too and then went out of the room.

***

I paused on the stairs and looked at some suits of armour and list of war dead.

I took a wrong turning and got lost as I went into the rooms on the first floor. I found myself surrounded by Vikings frozen in the act of alighting a longboat. Past them were display cases filled with maces and pikes, then Civil War helmets, torture implements, hand grenades, bayonets, chemical warfare suits and then, by chance, I found them.

There were now in a perspex box under spotlights and had grown like unnatural mushrooms, and sprouted and split the seams of their past.

The star and the swastika were pinned against a purple background and surrounded by three of my father's photographs. Above, the word 'Holocaust' had been printed in a gothic script. I looked around for the other photographs but the exhibition quickly dissolved into other things: Aboriginal clubs, bone necklaces, pottery, spice jars, brittle-looking skulls.

A group of schoolchildren suddenly emerged in an echo of laughter and chattering, led by a museum guide, who also had the word 'Holocaust' printed across her sweatshirt. Their teacher held the door open for them and told them to be quiet, sweeping her arm to motion them towards the exhibits.

I stood back and the guide corralled the children around the star and the swastika and told them about the Holocaust. The children listened dutifully and glanced at the photographs and then they were led away to look at pikestaffs and broadswords and a replica atomic bomb.

I wandered around the rest of the museum, idly taking in room-sized religious paintings and bronze statues and abstracts. I went to the café and bought a coffee and read a *Times* that someone had left under an empty cup. As I was finishing the crossword the children came in and slumped into chairs, clutching drawings of tanks and machine guns and pictures of crusaders and Romans that they'd coloured in. The teacher fussed around them, ordering certain children to be quiet as they ate their packed lunches.

After a while they left, crashing through the chairs as they went into the gift shop, the boys striking deals to borrow money to buy plastic swords and shields.

The girls from behind the counter came and started to tidy away the litter on the tables and I got up to leave. One of the children had left a drawing behind. On a piece of paper was a star and swastika; the star neatly coloured in yellow, the swastika green.

***

I met Jasmine outside the conference and we walked along by the river back to the hotel. We stopped at a pub and drank wine. It was hot and damp under the trees. We watched a barge filled with rubbish being overtaken by a pleasure cruiser, the slop and foam against the mud banks, pigeons swooping from one side to another. Jasmine was talking about the conference. I wanted to tell her about the museum but it would have come out wrong. Jasmine wanted me to test her French. She was going to Lyon in a fortnight with her undergraduates.

'You start,' she said and handed me her book.

'What should I say?' I said.

'Anything,' Jasmine said. 'Ask me about the weather.'

I laughed. 'No one is going to ask you about the weather in France. That's what the English do.'

Jasmine smiled and screwed up her eyes sarcastically. She seemed so much younger sometimes.

'Ok,' I said. 'Have you been here long?'

'Non, j'arrive hier.'

'When are you going home?'

'Je vais demain.'

Her accent was very good.

'Can you say everything in that way?' I asked.

'I've been thinking about that,' Jasmine said. 'I think you can.'

'What about *remember*?'

'I remember yesterday, I remember tomorrow,' Jasmine said.

'That doesn't work.'

'What doesn't work?'

'I remember tomorrow,' I said. 'How can you remember something tomorrow?'

'You could say that,' Jasmine said. 'It makes sense. I *will* remember that tomorrow.'

'But you're using it without the *will*,' I said. 'It's not the same. It's not a promise.'

'Well, I'll just have to make sure I don't have to say it then,' Jasmine smiled.

'You could learn that one,' I said. 'It's not hard just to learn one.'

'Come on,' Jasmine said. 'I'm tired.'

In the bedroom Jasmine fell asleep with her thumb jammed inside her French book. I packed the suitcase. Jasmine started snoring. I tucked her legs under the duvet and turned down the sound on the television. I watched the same news report again. And when it was over I watched boats moving along the river until they petered out and lights started coming on in the city. The moon rose vastly over buildings. The river settled into darkness but remained muscular and fast, rippling the lights from bridges and streetlamps and I saw the man from that morning rowing back across the water, battling against the ebb tide with the dog sitting solemnly behind him. Again and again the stern was pushed away and the man worked a single oar to bring it back. He seemed to slow in the middle, drifting ten, twenty feet downstream, his head bowed, exhausted, then he pulled himself a little closer to the other shore, before giving up again. I willed him to keep rowing and pressed my face closer to the window, then opened it, watching him thrashing at the water with his oars. The dog was barking. The man rowed on a little while longer but then, pulling in his oars, gave up his boat to the rushing tide. The swell dragged him further and further away and eventually he drifted under the shadows of a bridge and though I looked for a long time I could not tell whether he had made it to the other side.

Paintings on the floor

Michael is hanging up the paintings left against the wall of the newly papered dining room. Carla comes in and stops him.

"No," she says. "Leave them on the floor."
"Why?" Michael says.
"I read it in a magazine."

Michael climbs down the ladder with the painting.

"What magazine?" he asks.
"A Sunday magazine; a homes, interiors thing, you know."
"And it said to leave paintings on the floor?"
"Not on the floor, leaning, against the wall."
"Why?"
"It said that it gave the room an informal look, as if you are trying to decide where to put the paintings; it shows you are thoughtful and have an eye for details.
"I *am* trying to decide where to put them," Michael says. "Why do we want people to know that I *thought* about where to put them?"
"It's the act of creative arrangement," Carla says. "They have flower arranging competitions don't they?"
"Yes, but no one leaves the flowers leaning against the vases."

Carla shakes her head and walks over to the window.

"There's not enough room to leave the paintings on the floor," Michael says. "People will fall over them. In fact they will fall over them and ask me why they aren't on the walls."
"There's loads of room," Carla says.
"Oh, it's so pretentious," Michael groans.
"Luddite," Carla says.
"You mean Philistine," Michael says and climbs back up the ladder.
"What's a Luddite?" Carla asks.
"Someone who destroys technology," Michael replies.

"Well it's the same thing," Carla says. "You think anything original is pretentious."

Michael reaches into his back pocket for the screwdriver. "Oh come on, you hate it as much as I do, all that process over product stuff, it's tedious," he says.

Carla picks at flecks of paint on the window. "You like jazz," she says. "And Buddhism."

"Perhaps we could use our house to exhibit all our decisions," Michael says and begins to turn a screw into the wall.

He thinks about how this might be achieved.

He could leave the boxes of cereal out in the kitchen, or all his clothes on the bed, or all the videos scattered across the floor of the living room, or buy a hundred televisions and have each one on a different channel.

He thinks about the smaller decisions he makes from day to day, the decisions that he is not usually aware of making – where to look on the bus, where to scratch his head, the amount he has to open his mouth to eat, the amount of air to breathe. How would these decisions be conveyed?

And what about the more intimate decisions? Where to kiss Carla, which position to arrange themselves into on the bed, which breast to suckle first, how long to spend with his nose against her pubic bone, when to tell her that he loved her, when to tell her that he hated her, when to tell her about Helen.

The point is, he thinks, is that we choose and live by what we choose and keep our houses tidy. We like finality, he concludes, not a gallery of pending decisions.

But the paintings on the floor incident has made him apprehensive about telling her about Helen. It seems that Carla wants to know about decisions and he feels sick at the thought of having to explain the whys and the whats and the wheres, because he doesn't know the answers. Those kinds of decisions are made at some subatomic level. It'd be like trying to explain why water was made. It just happened. It still happens.

Of acid and water

The lights of the village woke him for a moment as they flashed into the car but once they were out in the countryside he fell asleep again. The painkillers were still working. In the darkness he seemed to fill the front of the small car. He slept with his head drooped away from her, making his shoulders into lumpy piles on top of his wide back. Watching him sleeping made her drowsy and an hour after the village she pulled the car into a lay by. She opened the flask of coffee one of the nurses had made for her and poured some into the lid. He rolled over and started snoring, and she got out of the car and quietly closed the door.

Standing outside, the night was clammy and she felt a warm breeze moving towards her across the fields that stretched away from the road, bringing the stench of cattle. She had been sweating in the car. Her clothes felt damp and her skin seemed thick and suffocated beneath. She heard cows lowing nearby and got the torch out of the boot to search for them whilst she drank her coffee. The beam was frail and washed the grass in a grey light, barely reaching the cows standing under the trees. They looked at her and when the light hit the back of their eyes they gleamed like glass. Then they moved away, leaving an old white bull nudging at the low branches of an oak tree.

She finished the coffee and shook the cup into the nettles next to the wire fence. The wind was growing stronger through the tops of the trees and it sounded like the sea. She got back in the car and switched on the engine. He woke, confused and frowning and looked at her.

"Sorry," she said and he looked at his watch and then at the wire fence and the dark fields outside his window.

She studied the bruises around his eyes and the bare patch in his hair that had been shaved for the stitches that ran down his scalp past his ear to his solid-looking jaw line.

"Do you want the radio on?" she asked. He shook his head and she pulled away through gravel and back onto the empty road.

"Have a smoke if you like," she said and he reached into his shirt pocket and took out a packet of cigarettes. The smell of vomit reached her. He'd been sick when they stopped for a drink an hour after leaving the hospital. She thought she'd got it all off his shirt but the smell was still there and he refused to change. He pressed in the lighter under the stereo and waited with his hand poised over it. When it shot out she jumped and he looked at her and pushed the amber spiral into the end of his cigarette.

The car filled with smoke and the smell of his clothes and his skin. She felt her head throbbing. She asked him to wind the window down and he ignored her and flipped through the paperback on the dashboard. She had bought it for him in the hospital shop but he had not read it and through the smoke she caught the smell of the fresh pages as he moved the book about in his hands.

"We should be nearly there," she said, glancing at the map on her knees. "It's stupid. I always seem to get lost. And I must have been there twenty times."

He stared out of the window at the black hedgerows flashing past.

"It's good of Holly to lend us the house, isn't it?" she said and he looked at her. "Did I tell you that the sale is nearly through?" He shook his head. "Everything's gone pretty much. The house is empty, Holly's gone. The new people are moving in in September."

They came to a winding section of the road that sloped downwards steeply through dense woodland and the paperback on the dashboard slid back and forth. She noticed him watching it and his jaw tightening as the book skidded to the edges of the car. Suddenly he reached forward, grabbed the book and threw it into the back seat.

She focused on the road and felt her hair sticking to the back of her neck. He winced and shifted in his seat.

"I need to go," he said.

She continued for another mile down the winding lane, trying to find somewhere to stop. She apologised over and over and he grunted with pain every time she dabbed the brakes when she thought she'd seen a place to stop. Eventually they dashed past a field gate set back from the road with a patch of lumpy grass in front of it. She put her arm around his headrest and reversed the car awkwardly, jolting his head against the roof and coming to a stop when the bumper met the gate. He looked at her and she got out of the car.

"It's alright," she shouted to him. "There's just a little crack on the brake light."

He opened his door and waited for her to come round. She stumbled in the deep tracks left by a tractor and undid his seat belt for him.

"Hurry up," he said and she reached around his back, pressing her cheek into his chest and locking her fingers. She moved backwards, with her shoulders under his armpits and he swung his good leg out and pushed himself up. He towered over her, lifting her suddenly and tipping her backwards. She reached out for the fence post she thought was behind her but caught the barbed wire fence instead and gashed her hand.

"Come on," he snapped and she held him steady while he unzipped his trousers and urinated into the long grass by the gate. Her palm oozed blood and she pressed it tightly to her jeans feeling a sense of elation; her miscalculation of his weight punished so quickly and violently.

When he finished he hopped to the car and fell into his seat. She leant across him and plugged in his seatbelt and then looked at the puncture marks that ran along her life line.

"Can you pass me a tissue?" she said and he flipped open the glove compartment and handed her a wad of napkins she'd picked up from the service station.

***

They reached the house shortly after midnight and she fumbled awkwardly in her pockets for the keys with her injured hand.

"Stay here and I'll open the door," she said and got out.
As she approached the door a light came on and a moth flitted around it. She opened the door and crouched to pick up the piles of mail and charity magazines in plastic wrappers. The house was silent and dark and smelled of damp. A clock ticked somewhere.

She went back to the car and helped him out. He held onto the roof while she opened the boot and took out the crutches the hospital had lent them.

"Can you manage?" she asked and he began to manoeuvre himself up the driveway. She ran past him and held the door open and he clambered up the three steps into the house.

"Shall we have a drink?" she said and went through the hallway to the kitchen, switching on the lights as she went, illuminating the bare wooden floors and the greasy looking wall paper.
"I want to go to bed," he said and she stopped and came back.
"There's a bedroom here," she said and opened a door to the right.
"It's small though."

He nudged the door with the end of one his crutches and she flicked on the light switch. They looked at the black iron bedstead that had a mattress and a blanket. He went inside and sat on the bed and put his crutches on the floor. He looked at her and then lay on the mattress, turning towards the curtainless window.

In the kitchen she found a jar of tea bags and boiled the kettle on the stove and drank the tea black in the living room which was empty apart from a sofa and a rainbow coloured rug in front of the hearth. The alcoves to either side of the chimney breast used to be filled with books but only a few tattered things remained, their spines cracked and sprouting wiry string. She took one down and sat on the sofa and flipped through the pages, which were brittle and yellow. It was an old encyclopaedia with very few pictures. Her eyes swam from concentrating on the road and she put the book back and turned off the lights.

She went to the window and watched the trees that surrounded the house moving gently under plum coloured clouds that looked like flesh.

***

The next two days were humid and it rained heavily. He stayed in the small bedroom at the front of the house and she read her books in the conservatory and watched the water streaming down the windows.

Outside, the garden was overgrown at the edges and filled with tall weeds. Holly was never really interested in gardening and once the house had been sold she mowed the lawn one last time and left it to tend itself. It became a haven of birds and squirrels and a feral cat wound its way in and out of the bushes at dusk and sat under the apple tree in the middle of the lawn

When the rain stopped for a time she managed short walks along the lanes near the house and had waded through the hip-high grass at the back of the garden to get to the little summer house, which filled with geraniums in little plastic pots that stank like urine in fur. There was an old cricket bat in one corner with insulation tape around the handle and a pair of shears that she cleaned as best she could and made a half-hearted attempt to cut off the weeds that had grown over the sundial outside the summer house and obscured any line that the gnomon cast.

She tried to study but she was easily bored and spent much of her time pacing the house, looking through the things that Holly had left behind or playing the piano that was out of tune and overrun with old papers and magazines.

She was rather surprised at the things Holly had left for the house clearance. In her bedroom all her dolls were still there, all her horse-riding trophies and the photograph albums. She looked in her wardrobe and found a rack of skirts and trousers and a rubble pile of shoes at the bottom. There were shoes still in boxes and she got them out to try on but remembered that Holly was much smaller than her. One shoe box was battered and dented and when she opened it she found the collection of shells they had made together during her first summer at the house some fifteen years before. She smiled and took the box down to the kitchen and held each of the shells in turn, cupping them to her ears, trying to remember what her youth was like.

***

On the third morning there was a thunderstorm and she decided that this would clear the weather and allow her to get to the gorge. Holly had taken her there after a storm during that first summer when they were young girls and they had watched the water cascading over the cliff and onto the rocks where trees, felled in the night, lay stripped of leaves and branches, their trunks long and white, like the spines of dinosaurs

She unpacked the equipment she had brought and laid it out neatly on the long table in the conservatory that she intended to use for examining her fossils. The hammers and chisels, brushes, files and picks were clean and unused and she picked them up and looked at them. She set out a pair of rubber gloves and then a large bottle of acid.

She thought about the lesson they'd had about etching fossils with acid and the elderly lady who'd burnt her finger in the classroom and had to be taken to hospital. Some of the other students said later that the lady had waited so long to be seen that she went outside and stuck her finger in the snow. It was February and it had been their last class and she remembered wondering what else she was going to do to pass the time while he was in hospital.

From down the hallway she could her husband shouting and she ran to his room, finding him on the floor, his crotch wet and a dark stain on the mattress.

***

By the afternoon he was asleep again, the mattress turned over and his trousers hanging over the bathroom door. She felt terrible and convinced herself that he had been lying there for hours screaming for her. She tried to read her books but could not concentrate and picked away at the scabs on her palm, trying to open the wounds again but they had healed quickly.

The rain had stopped and the conservatory seemed bright. She unscrewed the bottle of acid and put her nose to the top. It filled her nostrils and seemed to sting the inside of her face. Carefully she poured a little of the acid into a glass bowl and swilled it around and looked at it.

Then, scraping at the red marks on her palm, she put her hand flat into the bowl.

For a few seconds nothing happened but then the burning started and she gasped and pulled her hand out and held her wrist. She hurried to the kitchen and thrust her hand under the cold tap, her eyes welling up, her forearm throbbing as if someone had punched her.

Later her hand was bright red but the pain had subsided. The acid needed to be diluted; it had been too intense. The punishment needed to be prolonged. She needed to strip away the layers slowly and see and understand the process.

She experimented for the rest of the evening, dabbing small spots of different concentrations on her arms and legs until she started to shiver and had to wash the acid away.

Before she went to sleep she filled other bowls with varying balances of acid and water and left objects in them to see what happened.

The next day she fished out the objects and laid them on the table to dry. Most had turned to mush but some things intrigued her greatly. A carriage clock had become a disembodied collection of wheels and cogs and springs; a doll had lost its eyes and hair but its mouth had widened into an enormous smile; a shell from the shoebox had thinned to a white spiral that looked impossibly fragile, like a bone of the inner ear.

It was all a question of balance, she told herself. It was all a question of how much to destroy and how much to save, though she needed something more complicated than shells and plastic dolls; she needed something with bones and flesh and blood if she was going to learn how to strip her husband back to the layer she had known when she'd first met him.

In the garden she found a dead mouse, a piece of a sheep that the cat had dragged through the fence and a dead magpie with an eye missing. She wrapped them in a plastic bag and brought them back to the house, where, once they had been washed and dried, she slid them into bowls and tried to calculate the right amounts of water and acid for each.

She came back all day to look at the things lying in the dishes, desperate to take them out, but they seemed to be in the same state every time she looked and eventually she forced herself to go to bed.

When she came down the next day before it was light, the piece of sheep had turned to soup, though she hadn't expected it to last very long, and the mouse had been reduced to a skeleton and when she lifted it from the dish with a pair of tweezers it sagged and collapsed onto floor, the bones making no sound, some of them floating down like flecks of snow.

The magpie had lost all its feathers and they formed a crust on top of the dish, which she picked through until she found the bird beneath. A few sinews of muscle still clung to it here and there but mostly it was bone. She dipped into the bowl with a pair of tongs and gently eased out the skeleton. It hung limply but did not break and once it had dripped dry she managed to lay it onto a wooden board and spread its wings. She sprayed a mist of water over it and tiny beads stood out on the bones.

Once it was dry she felt breathless. Under the magnifying glass the bones seemed impossibly tiny, like fish bones or white hairs; the skull polished to the thinness of paper, and a buttery, opaque colour like the most delicate porcelain.

She moved the magpie's wings with the end of a pencil, feeling the resistance of tendons and ligaments and cartilage on the brink of dissolving. She had fished the bird out just at the right moment. Any longer and it would have fallen to pieces, something beyond frailty, an archipelago of bones turning on the surface of the liquid, dissolving and disappearing.

***

Later that morning she went to the gorge to search for fossils and left him sitting in the garden with a newspaper on his knee and his cigarettes tucked into his shirt pocket.

An hour later she came back with her canvas bag full of rocks and walked past him into the conservatory where the doors had been flung wide open.

She put the bag down and went outside. The glass of beer she had poured for him was still there and a wasp was curved over the rim with its head in the froth. She flapped it away with her hat and drew up a chair and sat down next to him. The iron chair was hot from being out in the sun and she felt it against her legs as she listened to the insects fussing around the tree.

"You should come to the gorge," she said. "It's so quiet. You can't hear a thing. It's so deep there's no noise."

She put the back of her hand against her eyelid and it came away with a smear of blood on it.

"I cut myself on a bit of rock," she said. "It's my own silly fault. I had the goggles in my bag."

She sat back in her chair and fanned herself. She could hear water trickling somewhere and followed the line of trees that ran alongside the nearest field with her eyes until they joined a large wood that stretched well into the distance and rose over a hill on the horizon made dusty-looking from the sun.

"Do you want me to read the paper to you?" she said.

Her husband made no response and she took the newspaper off his lap. Crossing her legs she flipped through the pages, trying to find something of interest or amusement as they used to do.

"Here," she said, "here's something" and read him a report about a priest who had crashed his motorbike into a war memorial not far from where they were staying.

He continued to stare across the fields and she watched his eyes flickering as they traced the movements of a swallow.

"Do you want a cigarette?" she asked and reached into his pocket. He raised his hand and pressed it against hers.
"I think I want to sleep now," he said and went inside.

***

She worked for the rest of the afternoon, chipping away at the rocks she had collected that morning and checking the enormous reference guides that her tutor had recommended she buy.

In the evening she heard movement down the hallway and a little while later her husband emerged in his dressing gown. She watched him walking across the room. He was still limping, though he could move without the crutches now. He went outside to smoke and when he sat down in the chair underneath the apple tree his gown flapped open and she could see the scars that went up his legs and ended at his groin.

When he finished he came and stood near the open door at the end of the table and looked at her. She looked back and then at the rock she was brushing.

"What's the matter?" she asked.
"There are some lights away over the fields."
"Cars, I expect," she said.
"They're not moving."

She got up and went to the open door and stood with him. They looked out across the fields at the lights on the horizon.
"See them?" he said.
"It's probably the village we came through on the way," she said.
"But the *sea's* over there isn't it?"
"No, it's that way," she turned around and pointed in the opposite direction.
"No it can't be. Every night the sun's set on the horizon there. That's west and the sea's west."
"No the sea's east from here," she said and looked at his confused face. "Did you sleep?" she touched his arm.

He looked at her hand on his arm and went back inside. She followed him and returned to her work.

"The doctor seemed happy that you were coming here," she said. "He said it was, what was the word he used? *Apposite.* 'An apposite place', he said. Do you remember we had to look it up when we got home?"

"I don't remember that."

"He was nice, the doctor, wasn't he?"

"He seemed alright."

"I meant when they brought you in. He seemed very, sure, about everything."

"I don't remember."

She bent closer and scraped away at the rock with a tiny pick. "Is *anything* coming back to you?"

"Some things," he said.

"What things?"

"Bits of things. Nothing clear."

"Like what?"

He took out cigarette and tapped it against his lips.

"The road," he said. "The road turning over. The sound of the car on the road."

She stopped scraping and put the rock on the table and stared at it.

"How did it happen?" she asked.

"I don't know."

"Were you driving?"

"No. I wasn't driving."

He looked at her and put the cigarette in his mouth.

"It doesn't matter," she said and watched him sit down awkwardly in a chair. She wiped her sleeve across her face and it came away damp with sweat. "It doesn't matter," she said. "Tell me another time."

He sat for some time with his head in his hands and his elbows on the table. He laid the unlit cigarette on the table and blew on it so that it rolled back and forth. Eventually it fell on the floor and he began toying with the fossils she had left at the end of the table.

"What's this?" he asked and picked up a triangular chunk of black rock.

She squinted down the table. "It's a shark's tooth," she said.

He nodded and put it back on the table. Then he picked it up again and pressed a fingertip against the point of the tooth.

"Please be careful with it," she said and he put it back.

"Are you hungry," she asked.

"No, I'm not hungry," he replied.

"You must be hungry," she said. "What have you eaten today?"

He ignored her and picked up the shark's tooth again and raked its tip against the wood of the table.

"Please," she said and he stopped and moved his chair closer to her.

"What's that you're working on now?" he asked. She looked at him and then back at the book.

"It's a laurel leaf, I think," she said.

"Can I look at it?"

She pushed her chair back and he came towards her.

Under the light of desk lamp she could see the stump where his thumb ought to have been and the white dent around his finger left by his wedding ring. His face seemed untouched though one of his eyes was bloodshot.

He picked up the fossil and turned it in his hands, and she tried hard to resist taking it from him.

He stared at it more closely and drew up a chair next to her.

"It's so flat," he said.

"It says in the book it's quite rare to find them so well preserved," she said.

He winced suddenly and rubbed his thigh.

"How's is it?" she said.
"Sore," he replied.
"Did you sleep?"
"Not really."
"It's too hot to sleep anyway."
"We should leave the doors open."
"I never sleep well here," she said.
"I never seem to sleep anywhere," he replied.
"It's always so hot."
"We should open another door so the draught gets pulled through the house."

She nodded and he looked at her.

"What happened, Michael?" she said.

He stared at the rock and then put it down and went to the open door.

"You must be able to remember something," she said after him.

He continued outside and lit the cigarette and sat down under the apple tree. She took off her gloves, closed the book and followed him.

The fields were dark now and the light from the house was a rectangle on the grass.

"Where were you going?" she asked.
"I don't know where we were going. We weren't going anywhere in particular."
"Then where had you been?"
"Nowhere."
"Nowhere?"

He started to shiver and she went inside and brought out a coat. He put it on and walked over to the fence that separated the garden from the fields.

"Who was she?" she said and he looked down.
"Does it matter now?"
"Yes."
"You said it didn't matter."
"It does matter. It matters a lot."
"It doesn't to me."
"How did you feel about her?"
"Nothing. I felt nothing."
"Tell me how you felt."
"Tell you?"
"Yes. Tell me how you felt."
"I don't know how to tell you."
"Try"
"I don't feel *anything*."

"How did you feel when they cut her out of the car?" she said and he looked at her then opened the gate and walked unsteadily across the fields.

She watched him disappear into the darkness and then went inside the house.

She stood for a while, looking at the fossils on the table and then picked up the bottle of acid and went upstairs to the bathroom. She turned on the shower and washed herself and then dried her skin carefully and methodically, rubbing the towel into all the folds and creases, working into her ears with the towel over the end of her finger. She threw a clean towel into the bathtub and soaked up the water and poured in the rest of the acid, which formed a thin layer across the bottom.

She turned on the cold tap and watched the bath filling up, trying to calculate the right amount of dilution she deserved.

He liked tap dancing and magic shows

Carla is trying to make Michael interested in the newspaper article about the man found hanging in the woods next to the motorway.

"I went to school with him," she says and rotates the paper so that Michael can see. "It makes you think doesn't it?"

Michael has his ear pressed to the speakers of a radio which fizzle out static. He turns the dial and tries to find some jazz.

"I mean, he's the same age as me," Carla says. "I wonder what made him do it."

Michael shrugs, intrigued by the French radio station he has found.

"I mean, what could be so bad?" says Carla and reads the report again. Michael sees that she is upset and switches off the radio.

"It says here that he liked tap dancing and magic shows," Michael says. "There's your answer."
"Michael," Carla snaps. "He's *dead*."

Michael makes tea and Carla returns to the newspaper.

"It's natural to make comparisons," Michael says. "When someone your own age dies you think about your own mortality."
"I feel so selfish," Carla says.
"Why do you feel selfish?"
"Because he's dead and I can only think of what it means for me."

Michael hands her the tea and she looks at the scenes of London on the mug.

"Look," Michael says. "Everyone assumes that everyone else thinks like they do. It's quite ordinary. He kills himself and you don't understand why because you would never kill yourself, which makes his death seem all the more unbelievable. I'm sure to him it all made perfect sense."

"Do you think I think like you?" Carla says and Michael thinks for a moment.
"Yes," he says. "Fundamentally."
"What am I thinking now then?" Carla says
"It's not like that," Michael says. "It's not telepathy. It's an assumption. It's why people can't stand one another. Intolerance is only a hatred of yourself."
"Did you learn that on your course?"
"Yes."

Carla looks at the man's photograph in the paper and realises that the caption under it is wrong. It reads – *vandalism in children's park*

Michael smiles at her and challenges her to a game of hangman. She slaps his hand with the paper and smiles back.

"English?" she asks.
Michael shakes his head. "Too easy," he says. "German words only."

Carla fetches the dictionary and they play a few games on the back of an envelope.

Carla catches Michael out with *Wurmfortsatz* and *Hodensack* and he complains. Michael gives Carla a fair chance with the word *Fluchtversuch* and draws elaborate gallows on a stage with steps and a tumbrel parting the crowd as she goes through the alphabet.

She can't get it. Michael tries his best to help but he comes to the edge of the envelope and has to start on the body.

The summer of the feral cats

The next day it rained for the first time in a month and once the girls had gone to school Rachel busied herself around the house, cleaning out the bath, the girls' rooms and then preparing the dinner, gathering fresh herbs from the pots outside the back door and making her hands pungent with the smell of rosemary for the rest of the morning.

After lunch she had a phone call from Francis Bone. It was the fifth time he had called since the funeral. He was tactful and polite; he asked her how she was and asked after the girls but Rachel sensed by the pauses when she replied to his questions, that he wanted to talk about something else. David had been with Bone for only a few months and Rachel had never met him in person. He seemed decent enough. David hadn't really said anything about him.

Then the reason for the call emerged. David's papers. Had she looked at them yet? She should not, of course, begin such an arduous task if she was in any way unready, he said, but they were keen to push the last work David had been involved in. As homage, he said, to David's estimable and unparalleled career. Rachel said that she would see what she could do.

She had been into David's study, of course, to clean and to dig out the insurance documents and policies for her solicitor, but her visits were always functional; she did not linger in the room more than she had to and she made the visits as bland and practical as a visit to the bank.

Yet the room smelled so much of him. His cigar smoke was a residue on everything – his books that lined the walls, the paper on his desk, the wooden box in which he kept his pens.

The phone call gradually ushered her into David's study. She had not been planning to go in there that day but Bone had set off a chain of loose thoughts that brought her to stand before the ticking clock on the wall with its pendulum swinging behind glass.

David had bought the clock in Prague. It was a dark, wooden Swiss thing, the face surrounded by a carved pastoral scene: shepherd boys and girls and sheep and vines and flowers. Once it had seemed so alive – so human with its little gestured narratives between the boys and girls and animals – but now it seemed that it was telling time for nothing other than itself, a purely mechanical thing that continued and continued in an unoccupied room, something that merely carried time through wheels and cogs and springs and other necessary shapes of metal.

Every hour a little door flipped open and a bird hooted twice and went back inside. It seemed so cheerless. But she hadn't the heart to switch it off.

She sat in the swivel chair behind the desk and pulled open each of the three drawers in turn, finding them stuffed with papers, notes, pages from magazines, clippings. And under the desk were stacks of paper, files and cardboard boxes. She had no idea where to start and she was only dimly aware of what it was that David had been working on; something about the Olmecs, she thought, or the Hittites, she couldn't remember. He seemed to be doing so many things simultaneously. She needed Bone to come here and do this. He would know what he was looking for.

Rachel looked out of the window and through the rain that moved thickly down the glass she saw the green shapes of plants and bushes and trees in the garden. She turned back to the desk and picking up the pen that had been left diagonally across a spiral bound pad, wrote the word *sadness*. She had to write it. Just to get that word out. To say it, finally. She looked at the word and sensed something shifting into focus inside her. She felt no pain, only relief that her sorrow had edged a little more into a recognisable world, and had meshed somewhere with language at a pace she could tolerate. She tore off

54

the piece of paper and looked again at the word she had written, satisfied and anxious, and then called Bone.

Late in the afternoon the rain stopped and Rachel made her way to the farm again, walking the path that led up onto the heathland above the sea and ran parallel to the water across six miles of wilderness and farmland before it came to the estuary which yawned across trenches and sandbanks.

As she rose above the sea the wind picked up and she zipped her coat closed, feeling elated at the coldness on her face. The sun was still high behind the drifting, isolated clouds that made the view alternately bright and melancholy. Darker clouds were on the horizon and when the sun came out, brilliant and solid, she could see a boat illuminated against the blackness, its sail very white - sharp and bowed like a scimitar.

She and David had loved it here. And even though he was gone she still loved the stillness and the light on the water and the taste of salt, the cloying smell of vegetation on the concrete sea defences and on the legs of the pier that were shaggy at low tide with brown wrack. She loved the way the flatness of the sea sometimes seemed to stretch an unreal distance and she was able to see the detail of clouds miles away, clouds that were depositing rain over Holland.

Passing the old concrete shelter that smelt of urine and sour fruit, she saw the farm below her: a small white cottage and a barn next to it, behind which two enormous sycamore trees rose and shaded the yard. The wind moved through the long grass in the surrounding fields and her eyes passed through square after square of land as she looked for the boy.

And then she found him walking along the lane that connected the farm with the main road, jostling three nervous cows in front of him with a bamboo cane. The cows slowed and chomped at the grass that spoked through the wire fence and the boy tapped at their backsides and they trotted along before slowing again.

She made her way down and over the stile that led into one field and then another until she reached the outskirts of the farm. She waited by the barbed-wire fence, staring at the back of the house where the windows were boarded up. Eventually, seeing no one around, she ducked under the wire and headed for the house where she paused and then edged around the wall to the yard. This was the part that made her feel the most anxious. There was a good twenty feet of open space between the house and the barn and although she was certain that the boy would not harm her if she was caught she still felt terrified at the prospect of some other person suddenly coming upon her, the boy's father perhaps, or some uncle or brother.

She waited by the corner of the house and then ran across to the barn and slid around the back to the hole. Her feet sunk into muddy clay and she put her palms against the barn wall to steady herself as she pressed her face to the corrugated metal and let her eye adjust to the gloom within. The boy was there, ushering one of the cows out of a pen and onto the concrete slab in the middle of the floor. Set into the concrete was an iron ring and the boy passed the end of the chain that was around the cow's neck through the ring and looped it a few times so that the cow could not escape. Then the boy took off his tracksuit top and opened the bag he was carrying. Rachel adjusted her position and swapped eyes. He took out a long knife and began to sharpen it vigorously against a metal file, making his rolls of flesh wobble and his glasses slide to the end of his nose. Once he had finished he wiped the edge of the blade on a rag and went back over to the cow. He walked around it and ran his hands over the hide. Then he cupped the cow's chin with his hand and tilted back the head, drawing the knife swiftly across its throat. The cow twisted its head away and the boy was unbalanced and stumbled. Its legs buckled and it collapsed onto its side, jerking. Its throat gaped like a sleeve.

Rachel felt her chest tightening. She realised her mouth was open and that her lips and tongue were touching the metal wall. The boy wiped the knife on the rag and knelt beside the cow, unfurling a canvas roll of slaughterman's knives and saws. Rachel looked at his massive back and the flesh that bunched near his waist. The boy took out a wide saw and crouching over the cow removed its head. Then he went away, out of her sight, and came back wheeling a trolley into which was set a large plastic trough.

Parking this next to the cow the boy threw the animal's head in and undid the chain from the metal ring in the floor before looping it over a pulley that hung from the ceiling. From the side of the trolley he removed a bucket, which he upturned and set on the floor, and an *S* shaped hook, one end of which he drove through the neck stump of the cow and the other he attached to the end of the chain. Wrapping the chain around his forearm he moved backwards and the cow began to rise into the air. The boy's muscles began to emerge from the depths of his flesh and Rachel watched them moving as he hauled the cow upwards and then tied off the chain in the metal ring. The cow began to revolve. The boy edged the trough underneath the animal and selected a claw shaped knife from the canvas roll on the floor. He stepped onto the upturned bucket and slit the cow from the neck to the groin, filling the trough with the things that fell out.

Rachel watched as the boy hacked off the cow's limbs reducing it to a bulky rectangle of bones and meat, an anxiety creeping up on her that it was getting late. Eventually she forced herself to look away and check her watch.

It was five o'clock.

The girls would be home now and wondering where she was. Ollie, the youngest, would be getting worried.

Rachel looked once more and saw the boy wheeling the trolley to the other side of the barn and she went home.

**

That night they heard sirens coming closer and looked up from the television as blue lights shuddered into the living room.

"I wonder what's happened?" Ollie said and went to the window and pulled the net curtains aside. "Oh," she said. "They're at the crossroads."

Rachel and Helen joined Ollie at the window and with their cheeks pressed against the glass they could make out the backs of the vehicles. Other people were also watching, standing at the ends of their gardens, or looking out of upstairs windows.

"Shall we go out and see?" Helen said.
"I'll go," said Rachel. "You stay here."

The two girls moaned but remained fixed at the window as Rachel put on her coat and swapped her slippers for shoes.

Outside Rachel waved to them and smiled at Helen when she placed her hands on Ollie's shoulders.

Down the road Rachel saw the last houses before the crossroads flickering with blue lights and the shadows of trees and people. There were two police cars and an ambulance in the middle of the road. A policeman was crouching by someone slumped with their face against the gutter. The paramedics were there too, the back of the ambulance open and starkly lit and filled with bottles, tubes and machinery. The person on the floor was mumbling.

"What happened?" Rachel said to a policewoman who was standing on the pavement.
"We're not sure at the moment," the policewoman said. "Do you live here?" Rachel nodded. "Did you see anything?" the policewoman continued.

Rachel shook her head and the policewoman moved away when her radio spluttered. The paramedics turned the person in the road over onto a stretcher and strapped a red blanket around them. Cars slowed down as they passed through the crossroads, faces peering out. The policeman put his hat back on and nodded to the paramedic who slammed the doors of the ambulance shut and got into the passenger seat.

The ambulance edged slowly across the junction and then disappeared. Rachel turned, walked a little way and then jumped when the sirens suddenly howled back along the street.

"What happened?" Ollie said.
"I don't know, love," Rachel replied. "Someone was knocked down, I think."
"Didn't they let you see?" Helen said.
"No," said Rachel and pulled the curtains closed. Ollie picked up the remote control and switched the television back on.

Later, the girls went to bed of their own accord. Ollie was dozing on the sofa before eight o'clock and eventually sloped off to bed; Helen felt a sudden wash of tiredness that the new school had, until then, kept from her with excitement and nervousness and did the same. Rachel was alone by nine and turned off the television and went into David's study. The piece of paper was still there and she looked at it again. It seemed rather meaningless now, no worse than that, *melodramatic*, a kind of feeble, romantic vanity.

Perhaps that was how it worked, Rachel thought. Perhaps understanding was a coincidence that could not be repeated exactly. There, that morning, the rain on the window and the clock ticking and the smell of David and the mounds of his papers had all met in the word *sadness* and then separated, and now there were no words she felt compelled to write.

Bone called again the next day but Rachel did not get to the phone in time and instead heard him leaving a message. He was apologising. About the papers: he didn't want to rush her. She should call him when she was ready.

Rachel felt guilty about her bluntness with Bone and went into David's study again. She became distracted by the books he had left on the desk and flipped through pages of photographs of prehistoric

59

axe heads, and bones scalloped into triangular knives, and twenty thousand year old handprints on the ceilings of limestone hollows, and paintings of spindly men surrounded by the smoky-orange forms of animals. Her eyes wandered over photographs of unearthed skulls and skeletons with Latin names that David explained to her once. She tried to organise some of his papers but could only think about the boy and the cow and eventually put on her coat and wellingtons and made her way across town.

The air was congealing with the expectant weight of rain and thunder, bringing out the musky smell of pine sap as she walked through the small square of trees and flowers around the war memorial. A man was there in a boiler suit trying to hose off the graffiti scrawled across the list of names on the pedestal, creating a dark water stain around the bottom of the stone. He looked up at her as she passed and switched off the hose and began to brush the water down the drains at the side of the path.

Out on the heath the wind was warm and every so often sunlight broke through the dark clouds and looking back as she came to the concrete shelter she could see the town's buildings lit up, dusty looking, the colour of cinder toffee.

Inevitably it rained and Rachel went into the shelter while it passed. Inside, it was warm and stuffy and a smell emanated from the litter on the concrete floor.

A newspaper was oddly, neatly folded on the small bench and under the seat she saw the three cats. She nudged one with the end of her shoe and its whole body moved stiffly. Poor things, she thought.

The cats had been a problem all summer and when a child had been bitten and taken to hospital the heath land above the sea was closed off and pieces of poisoned fish scattered in the high grass. A few days later, groups of men in boiler suits searched for the bodies of the cats and came back with their plastic sacks full.

Some of the cats had made it to the promenade and died there to be picked over by seagulls and, at night, foxes. Others were found turning in the brown foam at the edge of the sea with the weed and the polystyrene.

Returning from the farm the previous week, Rachel had found one lying in the shadow of the wall in her front garden. She called it a garden on account of the tubs of flowers that she had placed under the window, but it was no more than a row of paving slabs between the wall and the house. They'd bought the flowers, the girls and her, a week or so after the funeral. The buying of the flowers had coincided with the opening of the curtains, which had been shut since the burial at the request of David's mother.

She had let the girls choose whatever flowers they wanted and the flower pots were soon ringed by dark stains from the water they'd drowned the flowers with twice a day, trying to combat the heat that had made August long and sluggish. Many of the flowers wilted and Rachel gently pulled them out of the soil. The weeds between the paving slabs grew thick. The cat was lying in amongst the weeds, bloated and pungent, with brown ants in its fur and a milky pool around its head.

Kneeling down in the shelter now she studied the cats more closely. One of them looked like the one she found in her garden: a lean tortoise-shell with sharp teeth exposed by stiffened lips that made it look as if it were hissing. Rachel thought about the cat she'd owned as a girl doing the same thing when she made it sniff orange peel.

She felt sweat on her forehead and the smell sticking in her throat. She undid her coat and took it off and felt her blouse clinging to her skin. She went outside and found a branch under the tree and used it to pull the cats out from under the bench. They scraped through pieces of broken glass as they came and one dragged a soiled white sock with it.

61

Now that she had moved the cats she did not know what to do with them. They lay stiffly in profile, two-dimensional animals, their spines curved, their tongues hanging out like pieces of sliced ham.

She thought about calling the man who had come to collect the cat from her garden; the man who sweated and muttered and went away again with the cat at the bottom of a plastic bag. Like everyone else, he'd seemed irritated by the heat; in fact tension seemed to shimmer everywhere she went. The wide streets of the town, flattened by the heat during the day became sultry at dusk as the heat thickened into a width of breathless air that made sleep impossible until the early hours of the morning. And in these heavy evenings there had been fighting when the migrant workers, helping with the harvests on the outlying marshland farms, came into town to eat. Graffiti appeared over the summer on the sides of bus shelters and in the subway that ran beneath the roundabout in the centre. She had seen similar things before, years ago, when she was Helen's age, when it was the Indians they hated. Now it was things about the Poles and the Albanians.

But now in the last few weeks the weather had changed and the drunken holiday crowds had gone and Rachel started walking on the heath again. All summer it had been too hot and the girls had not wanted to go because of the cats. And this summer she had to think of the girls first. They'd coped admirably but Rachel was waiting for the grief to cascade upon the house like a tidal wave. She half hoped that it would. If it all came out before they moved then perhaps some of the pain might remain here and not follow them; the house might seal away the first agonising realisations of their loss. If whatever it was that was holding back the tears broke like a levee now Rachel felt she could cope. The longer they waited for grief, the more chance there was of the girls finding out what had happened. If it came to that, Rachel would be helpless.

She looked at her watch. It was getting late. The rain had passed now and the sun was ranging through the hawthorn tree and casting its shadow over the ground outside the shelter. Rachel covered the cats with the newspaper and went down to the farm.

She waited for an hour by the empty barn. The boy was not there and did not come at all. She was thinking about the cats. She felt that they had to be *dismantled*. That was the word that came to her. They looked too alive still and she could not bear to look at them so close to this possibility. It would have been the same with David. If she'd seen his body and it looked as if he was sleeping she would not have been able to resist shaking him until he woke.

She could do it to the cats, she thought. She could take them apart. She could do it like the boy did with the cows and the pigs and that mare she'd seen him shoot through the head as it struggled to deliver a breech foal.

Eventually Rachel went home. All evening she thought about the cats and about how she was going to disassemble them. She closed her eyes and imagined the cats' fur under her fingers and certain instruments in her hands: a hammer from the metal tool box in the garden shed, the axe that had been thumped into a tree stump behind the greenhouse, one of her kitchen knives, scissors, the bowsaw that David had hung on the back of the shed door.

The following day, Rachel stopped at the shelter and removed the newspaper. The cats were still there. She knelt down and swept the glass off the fur of the tortoise-shell. She pressed her hands on the cat's head and felt its skull and the tiny jaw and the teeth set into black gums, feeling a sense of growing confidence as the animals' mechanisms became apparent under her fingers. She felt how the bones connected to one another and found the joints to be fragile, the muscles were pliable now like putty, it seemed that they could be taken apart like animals made of plastic bricks, the pieces coming away one by one, cleanly, silently.

When she got to the farm she made her way to the hole and then after a few moments heard the boy calling and she saw him driving some pigs into the barn. He corralled them into a pen and swung the gate closed and leant on it watching the pigs grunting and scuffling in the straw. Then he looked straight at Rachel's eye. She was sure of it. And she instinctively jerked backwards. She waited for a moment and then put her eye back to the hole and saw that the boy was no longer looking in her direction but directing one of the pigs out of the pen and onto the concrete slab by pulling at its nose ring. The pig wriggled its head from side to side but the boy held it firmly and eventually coupled the pig to the ring in the floor with a chain. The pig squealed and snorted and rattled the chain. The boy went out of view and came back with a white plastic basin which he placed under the pig's chin. As he had done with the cow, he clamped the pig's jaw with his hand and pulled a knife across its throat. The pig spasmed in his arms, thrashing its head backwards. But the boy put his full weight on top of it and directed the blood into the basin.

The pig was hoisted onto the pulley and the boy got out his knives. He circled the pig, pressing his fingers against its flesh, patting its hind. He cut off its tail. Then he looked at Rachel's eye again. And kept on looking. Rachel did not pull back but watched as the boy put down the knives and walked towards her, past the huddled pigs, across the dung-covered floor to the wall where he bent down and pressed his eye to hers. He asked her to come into the barn.

Rachel edged in through the open doors and the boy was standing by the pig.

"You'll get a better view from there," he said and Rachel stopped where she was. The boy fetched the trolley and positioned it under the pig.

Up close, the boy seemed no more than fifteen, but tall, wide, his face chubby and hairless. He took off his shirt and removed one of the long knives from the roll. His flesh looked soft, like gently layered snow. Rachel tried to say something but it was lost in her throat. She turned to leave when the boy bent down but he called her back.

"Don't you want to watch?" he said. Rachel shook her head. "You wanted to watch before," the boy went on.

He smiled at her and she saw that his teeth were yellow and crooked. Rachel made to leave again but the boy banged the hilt of the knife on the bars of the pen and she stopped.

"Stay and watch," the boy said quietly.

Rachel turned back, came a little closer and watched the boy gut the pig, her head swimming when the innards filled the trough and lay there steaming. He hacked away the limbs and threw them in amongst the offal.

Rachel watched him slaughter three more pigs, scrutinising his clumsy but emotionless work with the knives and saws. He had a book open on the floor next to him as he worked, the pages filled with two-dimensional diagrams of pigs, their outlines like maps of island countries, sectioned off within as shapes and numbers.

"I got it off the butcher," the boy said, noticing Rachel looking at the book. "It tells you how to cut the meat up properly."

He struggled to sever a tendon as he spoke, but eventually it snapped and he removed a leg.

"It takes me ages to do it properly," he said. "All the muscles go stiff if you don't do it quick and then the meat's fucking useless. It's easier just to gut them."

He ran his hand over the pig's back.

"I should really burn all the hairs off," he said. "They use hot water, you know, in the proper places, to take off all the hair. And they give them this injection before they cut them to make them tender. It's all money, though. I only get a fiver for the guts and the blood off the butcher."

The boy took down the pig from the hook and sawed the carcass in half on the floor.

When there was one pig left, the boy stopped and opened a flask and poured himself a cup of tea from it. He offered one to Rachel and she accepted but did not drink it. Then he unwrapped a tin foil parcel and took out a slice of cold toast.

"You don't say much," the boy smiled.
"I don't know what to say," Rachel replied. "I shouldn't be here."
"I want you to be here," the boy said. "I like it when you watch me."
"How does it feel?" Rachel found her voice came suddenly out of her.
"When I cut them?" the boy said. Rachel looked back at him. "It feels smooth," he began, "when nothing gets in the way of the knife. I like it when I can cut the joints properly. Or do you mean when I first cut them?" The boy drained his cup and screwed the lid back on the flask. "It feels sad sometimes," he said. "It feels," he looked thoughtfully at the pig and swallowed the rest of his toast, "like you're a magician. One minute it's breathing and snorting and dribbling then it's lying on the floor like everything's disappeared."

Rachel lowered her eyes and the boy bent down and took out a clean knife from the roll. He offered it to Rachel. For a moment she was confused but then understood the gesture.
"No," she said. "No, no I don't want to do that."
"It's easy," the boy said. "I'll hold it down and you can cut it."
"No," Rachel said again. "I can't."

The boy laid the knife in Rachel's palm, while he climbed into the pen and hauled the remaining pig towards the gate by its nose. He nodded at the latch and Rachel opened it for him and he dragged the pig onto the stone. The barn suddenly filled with the pig's screeching and Rachel felt something cold rising through her head. The boy wrestled the pig to the floor and chained its nose to the ring. Rachel looked at the boy's flesh and the pig's flesh moving together, his wide, flabby arms encircling the pig's back and stomach.

Once it was tied, the boy backed off and the pig strained against its tether, wheezing, circling the ring, its back legs slipping. The boy beckoned Rachel forward and she came to the edge of the concrete.

The boy went back to the pig and wrapped his arm around its neck, his hand jutting the chin upwards. Rachel stepped onto the stone slab and then knelt beside the pig. She looked at its eye, its eyelashes, its patchy flesh with the white hairs, she saw drool hanging from its lip and the hairy snout twitching. The boy told her to cut it. Rachel moved uncertainly and the pig jerked backwards. The boy gripped harder and Rachel watched the muscles in his forearm pulsing and quivering and the pig's flesh doing the same. She smelt the boy's sweat and the pig's sweat, and the boy's breath and the pig's breath coming to her thickly, feeling suddenly tiny beside the wall of grunting flesh. The boy used his other hand to cover the pig's eye and transformed the wall into a tangle of different coloured flesh and limbs and sounds. Rachel did not know where to put the knife any more; the pig's throat was lost. She could not find it. She did not know how to find it. She understood nothing of the struggle beside her. It was something old. David had been visited by something older than he knew; something from the white spaces in his history books. Something primitive came to him that night on the Underground. It snaked through the tunnels blindly without recourse and found him sitting alone in the end carriage. It fell upon him swiftly, scattering his papers across the floor, knocking his glasses from his face, tearing at him, tearing, tearing.

When I brought you back to the North Country

Coming up from Rome, from Greece, by train

Waiting in the heat for your train at Bologna I watched a woman begging with a child criss-crossed to her chest. She made her way down the platform with a deck of cards in her hand. She came to me – I was sitting on the last bench in the shade – and asked if I was French. I replied I was English and she thumbed through the cards and gave one to me. It said: "I am poor and cannot afford to feed my child."

Then a man in a uniform came and ushered her away and she tried to hit him and the child kept on sleeping.

I will never forget your face as your train pulled in to the station.

Isn't this a beautiful ampersand?

I remember you drawing an ampersand all afternoon in Verona when it rained that day and we were stuck indoors in your aunt's place near the Teatro Romano. The cat that did not really belong to the house but used to come inside for milk was sleeping under the table.

We were sitting on either side of the kitchen table with your sketchbook in the middle and you were drawing a beautiful ampersand that looked like a hooked fish.

We had had that argument and were not talking but the ampersand indicated we were still an equation.

When I finished reading and you were drawing a particularly delicate curve I got up and went out in the rain, following the water as it trickled down the hill past the houses with the red roofs and into the

Adige, where the long legged white herons were looking for fish in the storm.

Milan

The rain followed us to Milan and it was dark when we got there. You waited for me on the steps at Centrale while I called Richard to thank him for telling me where you were. The taxi drivers were arguing with one another. A policeman stood with his arms folded by the entrance. There was that tall woman putting on lipstick in the reflection of the ticket office window. A man leant against the wall with a chessboard under his arm.

Richard recommended that pension on the other side of the city – do you remember the doughy mattress and the black and white television? - and we walked across the Piazza Duomo to find the underground.

The subway was full of warm air. I was watching you. You didn't know that I was watching you. You were rubbing your hands over your stomach slowly. I thought about the child inside hearing your hands like thunder.

The border

We passed into France during the night. You were sleeping with your head against the window. Outside it was dark and I tried to see where one country ended and another began but I missed it. I wanted to wake you and tell you how happy I was that we were on the train together and going back home. I wanted to tell you that I would give you everything; that I would fall upon you like a tidal wave.

Le Cirque at Aix-le-Bain

It was the end of the day and we walked through the carpark at the edge of the Lac du Bourget. It was August but the copper leaves and mist hanging over the water and the long sunlight made us think of autumn. At the far side of the carpark was a poster advertising a circus. It was torn at the corner and flapped in the wind.

You lifted the corner up and pinned it to the wooden board with your hand. We looked at the date and realised that we would be back in England when the circus began.

Do you remember how strange it was to think that everything would just continue once we'd left?

Christ in Lyon

We lost the view of the city and the two rivers as we went into the gardens near the amphitheatre. The trees enclosed us but the sunlight found its way through and spilled on the floor like snow. Then we came to the statue of Christ that scared us for a moment with his red heart behind his hand and his face looking down under the thorns. There was that couple kissing in the alcove beside the statue. He had his hand under her skirt and you laughed at them. Do you remember?

A bird in flight

It was when we were on the train out of Lyon that we saw that bird. It was a heron of some sort. The noise of the train made it rise out of the corn and you told me look to at the long legs trailing behind. Do you remember? I said that it looked like the letter y, an italic *y*. A *y* is like a bird ascending, I said. Or a person falling, you said, and drew one on the back of your notebook to show me.

Bastille

I remember the colours of the city as we stepped off the Metro at Bastille. It seemed as though Paris was made of ash. We found that hotel on rue Saint Bernard, the one Richard had stayed in. It was a Friday evening and the bells were clanging in the wooden tower of the church next door. We went up to the room in a metal lift which shuddered all the way and you undressed and took a bath while I leant out of the window to watch the men outside the café de Paluches. The evening was so warm. Do you remember, we filled the sink with cold water and put beer in it?

The sad streets of the eleventh

All the streets of the eleventh were so sad looking. Do you remember? All of them seemed so tired, as tired as you. All those shops filled with dusty furniture and iron machinery. And the courtyards set back from the street. So many people wandering. Africans in sandals talking loudly. That poor girl who argued with herself and pressed that bag of glue to her face all the time. And the rain washing into the storm drain outside the fruit stall.

I found you crying in the bedroom when I got back from the market. You wanted to stay. You didn't want the child. You wished the child were dead. Do you remember we had that long walk down the Boulevard Bourdon to the Seine and we talked and you saw that it was better to go home.

The Burghers of Calais

We were waiting for the ferry. You were feeling sick. I went and looked at Rodin's statue while you drank tea in that café with the harp in the corner. I took some photographs and walked by the docks for a while.

I didn't think you were coming but then you arrived and we boarded the ferry. And we watched the cranes and the dockside and the people getting smaller and disappearing.

The North Country

I lost you again when we got back to England.

When I found you it was an afternoon of leaves and bonfires and the smell of them in the rain. I walked down the older streets of the town where the streetlamps were fluted and peeling green paint and rolled at the top into iron scrolls.

I passed one house, the window of the front room crowded with greenery; the paisley- heavy curtains half drawn. Inside I made out a piano and a row of ornaments along the mantelpiece. No lights were on but I saw a man staring out.

I peered through the smashed window of the Methodist chapel at the wooden benches and the books and the silence.

A man, sheathed in waterproofs, rode out of the fog that was curling around the end of the street on a black bicycle and he was reflected in a large puddle further along the road.

I came to number eleven, the old schoolhouse, and knocked on the door and asked if I could come in. Just to be able to look out on the street from the inside of the house and look at the paintings you had done and watch you reading and the child sleeping in its crib. You said no and slammed the door. You thought I was a lunatic.

Cages

Joseph had slept on the floor outside Ebony's apartment all night blanketed by his coat and woke early to find a note in its pocket, instructing him to meet her later at Saint Germain des Pres. The apartment was locked but he thumped on the door anyway. A woman came out of a room along the corridor and told him to fuck off.

Even after what seemed to him to be a long, damp walk through the Tuileries, he arrived at the church an hour early and sat on a bench in the square watching the shadows as they passed back and forth between the trees.

People began to arrive for mass. Elderly ladies in dark coats came and shook umbrellas in the doorway. Men put out cigarettes and took off their hats. A woman arrived, carrying a heavy, square cage which bounced against her hip. In the cage, dressed in a clown's outfit, was a small monkey which toppled over rhythmically and bared its teeth when the woman stopped to push pieces of fruit through the bars. The woman said something to it that Joseph could not hear properly, though it sounded stern, and she covered the cage with her white headscarf and went inside the church, tidying her hair away from her face.

Others came and made their way to the church, pacing towards the entrance more swiftly once the rain started again. Joseph got up and stood under one of the trees but the wind churned the rain into waves that blew sideways into his face and he decided to go in and wait for it to stop.

The church was warm and smelled of sandalwood and dampness. The organist played a dirge and Joseph noticed the black-veiled women at the front. He sat at the back in one of the side aisles underneath a window that was alive with rain.

The priest emerged from a door on the altar and then two servers followed, one carrying a gold crucifix and the other a censer, pendulous in front of him. They walked down the nave and stopped at the front doors, where they turned and faced the altar. Almost immediately they began to walk back up the aisle and behind them four pallbearers brought in the coffin. At the top of the aisle one of the servers opened out a trestle onto which the coffin was lowered. Joseph could see the white pile of the dead man's face. One of the women began crying and another comforted her. The pallbearers bowed to the altar and left. Joseph could hear them talking too soon, swearing about their money and the weather that made them linger in the porchway, and every so often bursts of their conversation distracted him as latecomers arrived, creeping into genuflection.

The mass began and the congregation murmured their responses. A child began to whine. Joseph watched the woman with the monkey who was sitting a few rows in front of him lifting the scarf. She did her best to keep up with the rising and sitting and kneeling but the monkey's dampened squeals distracted her and she would remain standing when everyone else was kneeling or sitting when the hymns started.

He thought about Ebony and gazed into the structures of wooden rafters in the high ceiling, becoming distant from the mass that continued through him and past him, until the bells were rung during the consecration.

As the priest lifted the Eucharist, Joseph heard a screeching noise. He saw that the woman with the monkey had the top of the cage open and was trying to quieten it down by stroking its fur. A row of people turned and looked. The priest lifted the chalice and the bells rang again. The woman yelped and her hand came out of the cage bleeding, whilst the monkey jumped and ran along the row of chairs, hopping across the aisle and then along the chairs in the centre. People backed away and shrieked, or flapped their hands at it. Whole rows shuffled out into the central aisle and gestured to the woman who was wrapping the headscarf around her hand. She looked back at them blankly, then noticed a man drawing back his umbrella to hit the monkey and stumbled out into the aisle clapping her unbitten hand against her mouth, making sounds in her throat, as if she were trying to repeat and swallow the word 'mama' at the same time. The man put down his umbrella and the monkey leapt onto a woman's lap. The woman tried to scrape the monkey off her skirt and jolted backwards knocking down an elderly man behind her. A great noise erupted in the church, as chairs fell over and men shouted and the organist kept on playing.

Bouquets were trampled by terrified mourners and, startled by one of the servers lunging at it, the monkey skittered through a bunch of roses, shredding petals from the stalks. The monkey went out of sight and there was a lull as the central aisle became filled with people searching for it under the chairs. It reappeared on the coffin, sitting on the corpse's chest and then his forehead. Several of the mourning women on the front row shouted to the priest. Uncertainly, he moved towards the monkey and it leapt off, bounding up onto the altar, knocking the chalice over and throwing wine over the pursuing priest's vestments. One of the altar servers instinctively swiped at it with the crucifix and the monkey ran towards the back of the church.

Joseph could see it coming towards him and he half stood up as it leapt from the back of the chair in front of him onto the windowledge.

He felt the eyes of the church on him. The priest had been given the cage and he waited for the monkey to move again; the woman was mumbling at Joseph, gesturing for him to catch her pet.

Closer to him now, Joseph could see that the monkey's costume had become dishevelled; the hat was hanging over one ear and the suit was split at the seams. Quickly, it worked its paws over the hat and it fell off, a thimble on the floor. It looked at Joseph and he could see its fur being ruffled by the breeze coming through the half open window.

The priest began to make clucking noises and the monkey turned and watched as the priest waved a white disc in the air. One of the veiled women complained and the priest snapped at her that it was unconsecrated. The monkey jumped down and ate the host that the priest dropped on the floor, then another and another until it hopped forward and groped at the one inside the cage.

When the door of the cage was closed the monkey did not seem to notice and sat on its haunches nibbling at the edges of the wafer.

The congregation whispered and muttered and returned to their seats, righting them noisily as the priest, theatrically holding the cage aloft, walked around to its owner and presented her with it. The woman left quickly and as she opened the doors Joseph noticed that the pallbearers had gone.

He waited for the mass to resume before slipping out of the silent church.

Outside, Ebony was watching the retreating figure of the woman with the monkey hobbling across rue Bonaparte.

"What are you doing in church?" she asked when she saw him.
Joseph kissed her. She responded after a moment's hesitation and then put her arm through his.
"You seem angry," she said and he told her about the monkey.

They walked through the Latin Quarter, caught up in the crowds around Odeon and Saint-Michel and then headed down to the river. They spoke only to request or offer cigarettes. Ebony sat down at a table outside a café and ordered a glass of water when the bemused waiter came out. Joseph waved him away and they said nothing until the water was brought out.

"Have you made a decision?" Ebony asked.
"About what?"
"About whether you're coming or staying."
"I'm coming with you."
"We'll be gone for a long time," she said. "It might be better if you stay here."

"But that's not what I want. I want to come with you."
"What will you do while I'm at college?"
"I'll get a job."

Ebony began coughing and Joseph rubbed her back. She held up her hand and he sat back and watched a boat on the water knocking through the ice.

"I didn't mean all those things the other day," he said.
"Didn't you?" Ebony stared ahead.
"No, I didn't. You're right. I don't own you."
She continued to gaze across the river.

"I love you," Joseph said. She remained expressionless.

He touched her arm. "Don't leave me."

She turned to face him and he embraced her. She seemed satisfied.

They walked back to her apartment in the eleventh, underneath the dark arches of the canals and then across the expanse of the Place de Bastille, negotiating gaps in the traffic. She walked very quickly and he broke into frequent jogs to catch her up. The rain came again as they turned into rue de Charonne and formed coloured halos around the strings of Christmas lights along the street.

A little further down, the smell of baking corncobs lingered at the end of the dark courtyard, through which her apartment was accessed. Several gaunt looking Africans lounged around a deep, charcoal trough under umbrellas. One of them waved to Ebony and she stopped to talk to him. They went over to the far side of courtyard where a moss-covered bicycle leant against the wall and he gave her some money and she kissed him. The men eyed Joseph as he waited and then returned to talking or arguing, one of them attendant to the fire, beating the air above its smouldering heart with a handful of palm leaves, flattening the smoke, then letting it bulge upwards in slow mushrooms.

"Who's he?" Joseph asked as she closed the door of the lift.

"A friend," Ebony replied. "His name is Henri."

"Has he been before?"

Ebony stared at him and Joseph looked at the floor and then the lift stopped. She pulled aside the concertinaed door and walked onto the landing. Joseph followed and tugged at the door until it clicked shut and the lift disappeared. He took off his hat and coat and hung them over his arm.

"Don't make a fuss tonight when Henri comes, will you?" Ebony said.

"I said I was sorry," Joseph replied. "It's just hard to think of you with someone else."

Ebony unlocked the apartment door and went inside. Joseph waited for a moment then stepped through and, following Ebony's request shouted from the bathroom, closed the door behind him.

Guns and how they work

I find Chris in tears on the floor of the garage. He is surrounded by parts of my guns. He tells me that he was trying to find out how they worked and had taken them apart and got the parts mixed up and thought he might find the missing parts in the other guns and so on.

He has a system, though.

All the parts are laid out separately on the floor and he is trying to match them up to the exploded diagrams in the manuals he has open next to him, their pages oily from his fingers.

"One at a time, Chris," I say and he starts crying again.

I look at his t-shirt, which has a large number 73 on it and the word *Brooklyn* arching over the top. His mother brought it back from Greece last year. It was too big for him then and now it rides up his arms and onto his shoulders.

"Let's do this one first," I say and pick up the handle of a Browning.

Chris smiles and he sits down in the armchair and looks tiny again. His feet do not reach the floor and the magazines sticking out from beneath the seat-cushion are scratching his calves. He sits cross-legged instead and I look at the battered soles of his trainers. When he is settled he takes an inky-looking sandwich off a plate balanced on the arm and bites into it and then reaches for the glass of milk on the workbench.

"What's in the sandwich?" I ask and Chris opens it for me to see. He offers to make me one and, stuffing the rest of the bread into his mouth, goes off to the kitchen with a copy of *Guns & Ammo* under his arm. I look at the Browning and begin to pick out the parts I need from the scattering of metal on the floor.

There is a bee tapping on the window and getting caught up in a spider web. I watch it for a while and after going mad it seems to settle and then remains very still.

Chris comes back in with the sandwich and a glass of milk and I notice that he has washed his hands which means I am on my own now, I have taken over.

"Do you know what this is?" I ask and he shakes his head and hands me the sandwich. "It's a Browning. A GP35," I say and bite into the sandwich, which is thick with ham and red onion and cheese. "It's American," I add through a mouthful of bread. Chris nods and puts the milk on the worktop.

He watches as I reassemble the gun and asks me about the bicycle that is hanging from the ceiling. He wants to fix it up so that he can come and see me more often. He squeezes the tyres and spins the back wheel, which shudders and grates against the mudguard. All it would need would be some new wheels, he says. We could fix it up, he says, when we've put the guns back together. I tell him to put out his hand, which he does, and I lay the Browning in his palm. His wrist bends with the weight and he brings up his other hand and holds it steady – tiny fingers wrapped around the handle and cupping the underside of the barrel.

"Try and aim it at the back wall," I say and Chris holds the pistol out in front of him. It shakes and he lets it fall, laughing. He hands it to me and I hook it onto the rack.

He picks up the frame of the Beretta and asks me about the writing on it.

"1942: that's the year it was made," I tell him, "and the letters are Roman numerals for twenty one. That means it was made twenty one years into the reign of the Fascists."

Chris asks me about the Fascists and I tell him while I put the Beretta back together and then move onto the others – a Mauser, a Luger

PO8 with the long, sleek barrel and the Webley which, when complete, I give Chris to hold.

"That was your great-granddad's," I say. Chris weighs it in his hands and puts his finger on the end of the hammer. "Here," I take hold of his thumb and together we pull back the hammer until the gun is cocked. Chris smiles and I let go. "Pull the trigger," I say. He looks doubtful. "It's alright," I tell him, "there's nothing in it."

Chris aims at the back wall and pulls the trigger and the hammer snaps down. He tries it himself but can't pull the hammer back with one thumb and clamps the gun between his thighs and uses two. He pulls the trigger again and the snap echoes flatly under the corrugated iron roof.

"Look at the handle," I say and Chris turns the pistol over in his hands. He looks puzzled. "See the bit cut out of it?" Chris nods and runs his finger over the gash in the handle. "A German attacked him with a sword." Chris asks if his great-granddad killed the German. "I don't know, Chris," I reply, "I suppose he must have done."

He looks at the pistol again and says he is sorry for taking the guns apart.

"It's alright," I say. "It's traditional."

All the guns are fixed and on the rack on the wall. Chris asks me about bullets. He asks me if I have any. I go to the cupboard on the back wall and unlock it and take out a cardboard box. I show it to Chris and he opens it and stares at the bullets inside.

"Take one out if you like," I say and Chris puts in his hand and takes one. He rolls it between his thumb and forefinger and then presses the pad of his thumb against the tip and says that it is sharp.

"They used to be flat in the old days," I tell him. "They were called man-stoppers."

He wonders why they were flat.

"Well," I say, "They weren't exactly flat; their tips were dented inwards."

He asks why.

"When they hit you they exploded outwards," I say and demonstrate with my hand, starting with a fist against his chest and opening my fingers into a star. "They were meant to knock you down, not kill you outright."

He looks at his reflection in the surface of the bullet and I continue.

"If you get knocked down and injured then other soldiers have to help you, and if they're helping you they can't fight. It's quite clever really."

He asks me how fast bullets go.

"Depending on the gun," I reply, "they can go twice as fast as sound; faster than anything you could say."

Chris puts the bullet back. He asks me if a bullet can be used again if it's fired but doesn't hit anything. I say no, but I'm not sure of the answer, it's not something I've ever thought about, and I try to picture a bullet coming to rest on the ground like an aeroplane.

The bull

The three soldiers found the village in ruins.

They had seen many like this: roads pitted with huge craters, trees blown apart, houses reduced to low brick squares that looked like Roman remains.

Sometimes they found survivors or the buildings still smoking but this village was cold. There had been no fighting here for weeks. Bloated bodies lay on the main road that ran through the village and out into the country on the other side: a few old people too weak or too proud to run away, covered in autumn leaves and the grime splashed out of the puddles in which they lay.

Phillips prodded one of the corpses with the end of his rifle and the others watched; then they carried on along the main street to the church in the village square.

The front half of the church was missing – a bomb had come through the roof and blown the front and most of the side walls outwards - and the soldiers looked down the central aisle at an enormous pit in the floor from which the remains of pews, pillars and flagstones radiated. The roof of the church had collapsed almost entirely leaving a few rafters jutting into the sky, and the three soldiers watched as rainwater dripped from them into puddles and onto the painted statues that lay stiffly in the rubble.

On the back wall was the framework of a stained glass window, emptied of its colours, around which a fresco of angels had been fading for a hundred years. Beneath this, a huge, splintered wooden crucifix leaned precariously over the altar; one of the chains that held it in place had been ripped from the wall.

"There's not much hope for us if they got Him, is there?" Anderson said.

Phillips had his rifle up to his shoulder and was looking through the sight. He took it down and said, "What do we do now?"

Jackson, who was the senior in rank, told them to search for bodies.

Phillips went one way and Anderson the other, climbing onto mounds of rubble that extended into the graveyard where headstones had been shattered or thrown against the blackened stumps of cypress trees. The soldiers worked quickly, turning over lumps of concrete and brick with their hands, their rifles slung around their backs.

They found nothing living and moved further in.

At the front of the church they came across a piano covered in brick dust. Phillips flipped open the lid and dabbed at the keys. Anderson righted a triptych that had fallen on the floor and folded. He opened it out and looked at the paintings: Christ being crucified, Mary weeping, Christ ascending into heaven. Phillips noticed Anderson looking at the paintings.

"Do you know how fast Christ would have had to have gone to get to heaven?" Phillips said, playing the last three notes on the piano in triplets.
"What are you talking about?" Anderson said.
"They've worked out how fast you have to go to leave the Earth," Phillips replied.
"Do you think it applies to the Son of God?" said Anderson, wiping dust of the canvases with his sleeve.
"Seven miles a second," Phillips said. "That's how fast Jesus needed to go."

Anderson shook his head and as Phillips went back to the piano he began to follow the Stations of the Cross around the church, clambering over the piles of earth and stone. The first four were

86

hidden in the rubble so that the Passion began with Simon carrying the cross to Golgotha and continued until Jesus was nailed to the cross. Anderson studied the wooden carving of the slumped Christ and the women at his feet and the words 'Eloi, Eloi lama sabachthani' painted in a Gothic script below. He looked for the last two stations but they were buried.

"Come here," Jackson said and the two soldiers went over to where Jackson was standing with his rifle pointing down a hole in the floor.
"What's down there?" Phillips asked.
"The crypt," said Anderson.
"Look down," Jackson said and stepped aside so that they could see.

Half way down the steps a bull lay dead and the stone walls and the steps were covered in dried blood. The bull seemed to fill the stairwell and had it fallen any further it would have blocked the doorway at the bottom completely.

"Jesus," Phillips whispered.
"It must have wandered in from the farm up the road," Anderson said.
"Why would it do that?" Phillips asked.

They descended the steps in single file, stepping between the bull's broken legs and then clambered over its head. Anderson, who was last, stopped and put his hands around the horns. Their tips were covered in blood. Anderson touched the tips with his thumbs.
"They've been sharpened," he said.
"Why do they do that?" Phillips asked from the bottom of the steps.
"For fighting," Anderson replied. "It's a fine animal," he said and patted the bull's side, feeling the muscles hard like overlapping sandbags beneath the black skin.

The door at the bottom of the steps was open and Jackson stepped into the crypt with his finger poised over the trigger of his rifle.
"Anyone there?" he shouted. There was no reply. "Phillips," Jackson said, "bring that light in here."

Phillips took off his pack and undid the straps that held a storm lantern tight against the canvas. He gave it to Anderson while he took out some matches and then lit the wick and closed the glass door. Jackson took the lantern and bringing its light into the crypt saw the body of a man on the floor, his arms spread out, his eyes fixed on the ceiling, a shotgun diagonal across his chest. Jackson stepped over the body and with his neck bent under the low ceiling went to the back of the crypt, illuminating the shapes of stacked coffins and recesses in the walls where candles had burned down to coins of wax.

Anderson and Phillips lingered by the doorway looking at the body, their hands cupped over their noses. Jackson looked at them from the other side of the room and then came over.

"I don't know if it's him or the bull that smells the worst," Phillips said.

"Pick up the gun," Jackson said to Anderson and Anderson knelt down and took the gun off the man's chest. He broke it open and saw a single cartridge left inside and showed it to Jackson.

"Christ almighty," Phillips mumbled and turned away and Jackson and Anderson looked back at the body. An inch-deep ridge ran from the top of the man's left thigh to his right shoulder, crossing his stomach where the flesh at the edges of the gash turned inwards. Through the rips in the man's shirt they could see where his ribs had been exposed.

"Cover him up with one of those sheets," Jackson indicated a pile of shrouds that were heaped against the back wall and gave Anderson the lantern.

Phillips went back up the steps and Jackson followed him. Anderson put the lantern down and picked up the uppermost sheet and took it over to the body. He thought about putting the body in one of the coffins but did not want to search for an empty one. So he covered the body in the sheet and saw it was too short. The man's boots stuck out; battered farmer's boots with nail ends in the soles.

Anderson noticed the spent cartridge next to the man's body and picked it up. Then he went back up the stairs, stopping by the bull and lifting its head. A hole in its throat was plugged with congealed blood that smelt of soil.

When he got back up to the church Jackson was urinating next to the lectern and Phillips had the piano lid open again and was stabbing out the three chords that he had learned as a child.

And then the distance

The boy watched his father smoking a cigarette out in the snow. He had his shoulders hunched against the cold and behind him fields stretched away under brown clouds.

His father threw away the glowing butt end and got back into the car, smelling of smoke and coldness and bringing a swirl of flakes with him. He shuddered and pressed his palms against the heater vents. He twisted in his seat, looked into the back of the car and showed the boy his woollen hat: it was shaggy with spikes of ice and snow.

"It's not far now," his father said and edged back onto the road.

The boy felt clammy and sick and took photographs of the snowy fields through the window. The film came to an end and the boy wound it back before removing the cellophane wrapper of another disposable camera. He took a picture of his father driving and sunk back into his seat, drowsy from the heat now pouring out of the vents. The radio was on low and voices and music reached him indistinguishable from one another.

They fell behind a tractor and rode in the trenches that its trailer made in the snow. It threw up a spray of sludge that the wipers moved away in thick slabs.

"Look John," his father said and the boy leant forward and looked at the cow that was peering out of the back of the trailer. The boy rested his elbows on the front seats and watched the cow licking its eye.

A mile later the tractor slowed down and went through an open gate into a field of frozen mud. The boy watched as the tractor came to a halt at the top of the field and the farmer opened the door of the trailer. The cow's head poked out and the farmer led it unsteadily down the wooden gangway into the field. The boy saw its breath clouding and then the field was gone.

Eventually the road came to an end and beyond the concrete bollards the leaden sea spread out towards a dismal horizon swept by snow clouds. His father pulled into the side of the road and stopped.
"Wait here," he said and got out of the car. The boy watched as his father clambered over a stile built into a dry stone wall next to the road. A moment later he reappeared and gestured for the boy to follow him.

The boy slipped and skidded on the steps and at the top of the stile he could see his father wading across a field towards a caravan that seemed buried in the snow. He climbed down the other side and followed his father, feeling the coldness of the snow on his crotch.

Underneath the caravan was a dark patch of grass, and water dripping from the roof had congealed into an enormous beard of ice that covered a window.

Inside the caravan a smell of fruit and sweat was held in the air by the cold. His father was kneeling on the floor fiddling with a gas heater. There were two beds separated by a foot wide gap that was filled with books and cardboard boxes and a battered looking bass drum lay on one of the beds.
"Did Callum play that?" the boy asked.
His father looked up momentarily. "No, he let his dog sleep in it," he said and the boy looked inside and saw a blanket covered with hairs.

Eventually the gas fire was lit and the caravan began to warm up.
"Are you hungry?" his father said. The boy nodded and his father went out to the car and returned with a box filled with tins and bottles and his camera bag slung over his shoulder. He opened a tin of spaghetti and emptied it into a pan which he set onto the one ring cooker in the corner. The boy sat on one of the beds and watched his father stirring the spaghetti with his gloves on. His father looked at him and smiled.

"Can I call Mum?" the boy asked. His father put the tip of the spoon to his lips and turned off the gas.

"You won't get a signal up here," he said and scraped the spaghetti out onto a plastic plate.

"Do you think she's alright?" the boy asked.

His father folded a newspaper in half and put it on the boy's lap and then gave him the steaming plate. "I'm going to have a sleep now," he said and got into the other bed and pulled up the hood of his anorak.

The boy ate the spaghetti and then went outside.

It had stopped snowing and the air was still. He found a path down from the field to the beach through the snow covered sand dunes and walked towards the edge of the sea, his presence raising a flock of wading birds that lifted off simultaneously as he approached them. He looked out at the sea and thought about his mother and walked for an hour along the shoreline listening to the waves breaking and the sound thudding against the dunes.

He saw nothing else apart from a fishing boat way out in the grey distance, its light winking feebly. Snow came in flurries, dissolving into the sea or patting gently down on the drifts that had heaped up against the huts dotted along the shore.

Through the still air he kept hearing the call of a bird that was a different sound to the burbling waders. He passed a huddle of ancient-looking tractors and flaking rowing boats and eventually found a hawk tethered to an upright post of a rotten groin.

He looked about but saw no one. The hawk watched him and then looked at the sea. The wind ruffled the feathers around its neck and bells jangled as it pecked at the moss and black seaweed under its feet. The boy looked at the smooth curve of its beak and thought about the things it might have caught in the sharp, yellow tip. The hawk opened its mouth and shrieked and the boy saw its grey tongue. He moved forward slowly but the bird pushed itself into the air, trying to fly away; the rope tightened and yanked the hawk into a distressed arc that tumbled out feathers before it thumped awkwardly into the sand and then flapped back to the post.

The boy picked up a feather and ran back to the caravan and saw that his father was still sleeping. He put the feather under his pillow and lay on his belly and flicked through some of the books on the floor beside him: a *Guinness Records* book and a book about the islands that were apparently off the coast somewhere in that grey sea. Another was about birds. He tried to find a picture of the hawk but nothing seemed to match. The last book was an atlas and the boy opened up the page he thought they were on and tried to find the names of the towns through which they had passed. He heard his father stirring and then he looked over at the boy.

"Where are we?" the boy said. His father wiped his eyes and nose and sat up on the bed. He held out his hand and the boy handed him the atlas. His father shuffled aside and the boy went across and sat with him.

"We started here," his father said and pressed his finger over north London. "We went up here" he traced the blue line of motorways, turned the page and continued upwards past Carlisle, Glasgow, over thinner lines that wriggled between the crinkles of mountain ranges, until he stopped at the edge of the coast.

"What happens if we keep going?" the boy asked.

His father moved his finger on a straight line northwards and turned from page to page.

"Do you know," he said, "if we kept on going we wouldn't really hit another bit of land until the South Pole."

The boy wanted to see for himself and following the same route as his father he found that, barring a lump of Greenland, which was probably only ice anyway the boy thought, their journey's momentum would curve over the North Pole before slicing cleanly through the Bering Straight and into a twelve thousand mile line that ran between specks of islands across the Pacific to Antarctica.

"I'm going outside for a cigarette," the man said. The boy moved to let him past and began to scrutinise the remote places of the world, trying to imagine what it was like to live there and look out at the sea, and how where he was now was someone else's distance.

After a few minutes his father came back inside and collected his camera.

"I'm going to walk up onto the cliffs and take some pictures," he said. "Are you coming?"

The boy put the book down and buttoned up his duffle coat and followed his father out of the field and onto the cliff tops.
"Stay on this side of me," his father said. "Sometimes the snow sticks out over the edge and you can fall right through it."
The boy moved and walked next to his father's right side, trying to keep up with him, looking behind and seeing the moment of his warning etched into the snow, where a set of small footprints veered away from the edge. His father stopped and snapped at the undulating mounds of snow and at the sea.

They walked on a little further, passing the shapes of trees that against the white sky looked like the innards of lungs. Lonely looking birds circled above and a few seagulls were out in the grey sea bobbing on its surface or diving.

"When can we call Mum?" the boy asked. The man looked at him and then fiddled with his camera.
"Later," he said.

The man put his camera away and they turned back to the caravan, walking in the holes they had made earlier. The boy heard the hawk calling again but said nothing.

As they got back to the road the man handed the keys to the caravan to the boy and they boy climbed over the stile and the man walked the other way to the pub in the village a mile down the road.

Back in the caravan the boy read more of the books on the floor and held the hawk's feather in his hands and felt its texture between his fingers.

His father did not return until it was dark and the wind caught the door as he opened it and slammed it against the caravan's wall.

"The weather's coming in," his father said and locked the door behind him. The boy went back to his book as his father fiddled with the radio, which produced a whistling sound that occasionally swooped into crackling speech. His father pressed the set against his ear and finally tuned it to the shipping forecast. The boy heard a suppressed voice reeling off a list of names and numbers. He started to say something but his father waved his hand at him to be quiet.

"There," his father said, "that's us: Fair Isle. I asked the man in the pub. Gale force eight."
"Is that bad?" the boy asked
"I don't know."

They ate a tin of potatoes and mince and the boy buttered some slices of bread which they used to wipe up the gravy left on their plates. The boy watched his father's face in the lamp light.

'Can we call Mum tomorrow, then?' the boy asked.
'There's a phone in the pub. We'll call her from there,' the man said.
'Will she talk this time?'
'She might.'
'I want her to talk.'
'Your mother's not well yet. She doesn't always know what's going on.'
'When will she be better?'
'Soon.'
'Does she speak to you?'
'Sometimes.'
'What does she say?'
'She asks about you.'
'What does she ask?'

'If you're alright. She does love you, you know.'
'Can't we call her now?'
'I told you. We can't get a signal here. Get some sleep now.'

The boy wiped his eyes and his father leant over and kissed him on the forehead. The boy saw his own shock manifest itself in his father's face, which seemed to sag suddenly and firm into a heaviness that lasted until the boy fell asleep, focused on the cold, damp stain above his eye.

That night the boy woke to the sound of the wind buffeting the caravan. His father was gone. The boy thought about the hawk and what it would do in such a storm. He heard something scraping against the side of the caravan and he looked between the curtains to see a herd of cows moving past in the blizzard, their hides steaming.

An hour passed and his father had not come back. The boy dressed and went to the door. Snow was flying horizontally across the field and he could see trees swaying wildly in the darkness. He closed the door and went towards the road. The car was still there, buried under snow.

He walked down to the beach and felt the sand shuddering beneath him. Black waves towered and thundered. He called out for his father. He walked along the sand, blasted by the spray and wind and climbed up onto a mound of rocks and called out again into the black sea that seemed to undulate and become part of the sky. And the boy thought of all the space there was beyond him, all that ocean and ice, the horizon and then the distance, and how it all seemed to be falling on him.

He heard a sound in the air. The hawk appeared above him and shuddered down through the gale onto a rock. It moved awkwardly and the boy saw that the end of its leg was mangled where the foot should have been. The hawk blinked and looked at the boy and then rose into the wind and was thrust upwards.

It held the world in its eye: the rocks, the shape of the sand, the endless plain of the sea, snow covered fields, roads, lights of villages, higher now, seeing the ragged coastline, leaving the speck of child behind as part of the darkness, rising into wisps of vapour, then swallowed by a snow cloud as thick as sleep.

Carla is crying

Carla is crying because she has a dying snail on her lap. She is not crying because the snail is dying but because the snail is leaking onto her only expensive dress. Michael suggests that she replaces the tissue on which the snail is lying and she carefully leans forward and flips down the glove compartment where she finds a wad of napkins.

"What are you going to do with this fucking thing anyway?" Carla snaps and rolls the snail onto the fresh napkin. She holds the old tissue by one corner. It has a stain on it the colour of motor oil.

"I don't know," Michael says and winds down the window.

"It's not as if you can give it a saucer of fucking milk is it?" Carla says and Michael knows she is upset because she has sworn twice in the last two sentences.

"Look, I don't know what I'm going to do with it," Michael says and looks at the greasy stain on Carla's white dress. "I'll put it in the garden or something."

Carla looks out of the window, but keeps one eye on the snail, worried that the bumpy country road will knock it off the napkin and onto the floor and necessitate her picking up. She feels sick at the thought of touching its skin – a cold, dead tongue – and at the thought of the cracked shell leaking clear glue all over her fingers.

"I don't know why you're so fucking upset about it," Carla says. "Snails get stood on all the time."
"I know," Michael replies, "but I was angry about what you said before and I think I *wanted* to stand on this one when I saw it."

Carla looks at the snail's horns moving in and out and thinks of mud and spots of ink in water.

Michael thinks about eating snails. He thinks that they might have the texture of strawberries. Michael cannot bite into strawberries, the texture makes him feel sick and so he has to mash them between his tongue and the roof of his mouth.

Perhaps it would be the same with snails.

Pearls melt in vinegar

The man put his arms around the girl in the wheelchair. She put her arms around his neck. They were both fat. They joked about that a lot. The man locked his hands together at the small of her back and leant backwards to lift her into the car. She hung from him heavily.

They drove away from the supermarket towards the man's home. The girl wanted to talk.
"Did you see the butterfly?" she said. The man shook his head.
"No, I didn't see it," he said.
"It was when you were in the toilet," she said. "It was fluttering about by the doorway and its wings kept opening the doors."
"It might have been people," the man said.
"No, no it was the butterfly," the girl insisted. "There were no people, not all the time."

The girl wiped her forehead with the back of her hand.

"Did you know that butterflies can't fly if it's too cold?" the man said.
"Why's that?" the girl said.
"Their wings don't work if it's too cold. They're warm blooded or cold blooded. I can't remember which."

The girl fanned herself with the road atlas from the dashboard.

"Tell me some new ones," she said. She liked facts. He was full of them. He learnt them from a book. She tried to learn them too but she couldn't remember them properly.

"Did you know that more people are killed by donkeys than in plane crashes?"
"Heard it," the girl said before he'd finished and they both laughed.

The man thought for a second.

"Did you know that a cockroach can live for weeks with no head?"

The girl pretended to retch. She always did that when he mentioned insects.

"Did you know that paper can't be folded more than seven times in half?"
"Oh come on," the girl said, "you're scraping the bottom of the barrel now."

The man laughed and she felt like she loved him.

"OK," he said, "did you know that every time you lick a stamp you're getting a tenth of a calorie?"
"That's a good one," the girl said.
"So you can eat as many stamps as you like," the man said.

She liked it when he joked like that.

He couldn't think of any more and they became quiet for a while.

They stopped at a red light outside a school. The girl looked at the children playing behind the railings.

"Tell me what you did when you were young," the girl said. "When you were my age."
"How old are you?" the man said and the girl pulled a face at him. He knew how old she was. He was always joking with her.

"What do you want me to tell you about?" the man said.
"Tell me something amazing," the girl replied and turned the air vent towards her face. It was very hot in the car.

The man thought for a moment. He knew what he was going to tell her, but not how he was going to say it.

"I had a friend," the man said.
"I don't want to know about your friend," said the girl snappily.

"It's about me *and* my friend," the man squeezed her knee and she yelped. He was always joking with her.

"My friend's mother died you see," the man began. "We were only seventeen or so, I suppose. And his mother died. Very suddenly."

The lights changed and the girl watched him set off again and felt the cool air blowing on her face.

"He turned up on his brother's moped one day and asked me to go out with him. I went, of course. Only I didn't have a helmet so I had to use a saucepan with a belt wrapped around it under my chin. Anyway, we went down to the wasteground. It's not there now. There are houses. And Harry went up and down this path and over some bumps a few times, and then we drove up off the wasteland and went to the cemetery."
"What did you go there for?" the girl asked.
"I'm getting to that bit, silly," the man said and the girl stuck out her tongue. "We sat under a tree and Harry was saying all these terrible things about his mother."
"Like what?" the girl said.
"I don't remember now. He was angry with her, I suppose."
"And?"
"And so we waited until this hearse came along. I think it was the first time I'd ever seen one close up."
"I think they actually *look* like death, don't they?" the girl said.
'How do you mean?'
'I don't know,' the girl said. 'They just seem all black and serious, don't they?'

She watched him thinking about this and he seemed to agree with her.

They waited at a crossroads and then turned right by the cathedral, the road dabbed with sunlight coming through the trees. The man continued.

"So, all these people got out and the undertaker and his men got the coffin out of the back and carried it up to the grave. I remember there was this woman who kept on yelping like a little dog. She was crying but it sounded like a dog."

"Go on," the girl said.

"Well, we waited until all the people had gone and then Harry and me wheeled the moped up to the hearse and Harry got out this rubber tube and opened up the petrol cap on the hearse and stuck one end of the tube into the tank."

"What for?"

"So he could suck out the petrol."

"Ugh."

"He got a mouthful almost right away. Then it started gushing out and we jumped back on the moped and left a great puddle underneath the hearse."

The girl looked at him.

There," he said. "That's it. It's not amazing is it?"

"What did he do all that for?" the girl asked.

"He thought he could stop people being buried."

"That's stupid," the girl said. "People have to be buried."

"Well, I suppose he thought that if they couldn't bury anyone, then no one could die."

"That's even more stupid," the girl said. She was really sweating now. There were dark patches on her clothes.

"We were only seventeen," the man said. "You don't think straight when you're seventeen."

The girl thumped him on the arm and then turned on the radio. He touched her hand and she leant over and kissed his face.

"Did that really happen?" she said. "Did you make all that up?"

"It really happened," the man said.

"What does petrol taste like?"

"Old coins," the man said.

"How do you know?"

104

"Harry told me," he said.

"I want to be buried," the girl said. "I can't stand the thought of being burned."

"We could get you frozen," the man smiled. She thumped on the arm again. He was always joking with her.

"They do coffins with telephones in now, you know," she said.

"What for?"

"In case they bury you alive. I can't stand the thought of being buried alive either."

"You're a taphephobe, then," the man said.

"A what?" the girl replied.

"You're afraid of being buried alive."

"Well, make sure you get me a coffin with a phone inside then," the girl said.

"Who pays the bill?" the man asked. The girl smiled at him and he went on. "Is it only for outgoing calls? Would you hear it ringing if there was no oxygen? I hope no one can dial in because you can bet your life it wouldn't be long before someone'd be trying to sell you a kitchen."

The girl shrieked with laughter. The man smiled. She felt so happy, being with him in the car and joking about death and coffins like that. It made it alright. It stopped her being scared. It was like when they joked about being overweight. It made it alright.

It was like when he lay on top of her in the night and she felt like she was drowning under his body and his breath and his lips. It was alright because she wasn't scared of death anymore.

"Did you know that Shakespeare invented the word *elbow*?" the man said. She smiled at him and shook her head.

It was alright drowning in him. She couldn't be afraid of death anymore when it whispered in her ear about how much she was loved and how much she was needed and how nothing would ever happen to her.

"Did you know that pearls melt in vinegar?" the man said and the girl thought about it, picturing the pearl dissolving beautifully into an iridescent, glossy milk.

Tell me again about the thunder

When I think of her I think of thunder.

It always seemed to be there in the background, in the summer, when we came to see Michel. She would leave his apartment early in the morning and sit by the river and paint. I would wake later, find her missing and, after a long breakfast, set my typewriter on a chair on the balcony and try and write.

The afternoons would end in a milky haze and rain would follow, bringing thunder. And she would return with her easel under her arm, her clothes sagging, her glasses misted over.

All my novels have thunder in them. The more developed work has only the suggestion of thunder; the weaker narratives always start with thunder and get no further, so that the story is no more than a clumsy crescendo, which seems out of place, the wrong end of the novel.

A thunderstorm had lumbered over Paris for a second night, more violent than the first, close and muscular. The clipped shadows that had rested next to buildings in the bright afternoon, under linden trees in quiet squares, under the shapes of people lounging by the river were absorbed into a larger kind of darkness that the early evening brought. In heavy movements daytime heat, now rising from the stone and steel that had absorbed it, was folded back by low clouds until it broke under its own weight in long reverberations over the city.

I was caught in a downpour on my way back from the cemetery. My coat hung by the door, dripping onto the linoleum, mimicking the typewriter on which I was trying to coax two characters into life from rhythm, ink and paper. The cemetery is not all that far from Michel's apartment but I stayed longer than I had intended to. I'm not sure what to do there anymore— I never talk to her now. I just sit and stare at the stones feeling anaesthetized. It used to be different. I used to talk. I used to bring flowers.

Michel is always away on holiday now during August so he lends me his place. He leaves the keys with the man next door, the ancient Monsieur Blanc, who fixes clocks and speaks no English. The first time I came to stay, Monsieur Blanc called the police out of sheer confusion.

Wracked with the nostalgia that seems to afflict middle age, Michel wants to sell his apartment and move back to Montpelier, where he was born, but he keeps it so that I have somewhere to stay when I come for her anniversary. I tell him that I want him to sell, but he knows I am lying.

Coming here seems to stir up a creativity that London dampens down and I write as much as I can. I wander the city, as far as my age allows, eat good Egyptian and Moroccan food in the places still open, but mostly write.

I write fiction. Fictions. Novels. Never poetry. Not now. It seems so worn. Poetry is the language of first meetings and swift partings; the language of human distance, and the yearning that invigorates and wearies lives that linger precariously between union and loneliness. She stopped being moved by my words once we married. They got too familiar.

Two characters have visited me persistently for the last few months and have grown as my restlessness has grown. They are reluctant to *mature*, however. They have grown only into monsters of fiction, shapeless and huge. They drip over the edges of the page. They will not stick. They will not *become*. All I can offer them are moments, situations, gestures. They are man and woman but they are not representative of her and me. They are the two strands of a feeling which has been gestating in London throughout the spring.

Late in the night a warm breeze, wet with the rain, blew along Rue Amelot and pushed through an open window of the Hôtel Papillion making the curtains bulge into the room. They touched the face of the woman who was standing there with her eyes closed, trying to cool herself in the hot suffocation that filled every pore of the city. Her husband watched her from the bed, watched the curtains brushing against her face and partially enveloping her body in white waves. The room lit up twice, silently. A few seconds later, the thunder sounded flatly once against the darkness before its heaviness was emptied through the August night.

I try to write in London. I sit and tap at the keys at night. I read something. I look at something that belonged to her. I feel anxious. I miss her. I don't miss her.

I try to write in Paris. I sit and tap the keys at night. I get up. I walk around Michel's apartment. I press the keys of his piano and try to hear the sounds as long as I possibly can.

It is twenty years since she died. She seems everywhere, and yet absent from everywhere.

"Come and lie down with me," the man held out his hand for a few seconds, virtually touching her as the room was so small, but when she did not respond he withdrew it and tapped the end of a cigarette on the flat of a closed paperback. He glanced up at her figure by the window – her brown hair tied back from her face, the short red night-gown, the pale skin beneath it. He opened a book of matches that had the name of the hotel on them and worked one free. He looked at her again. She had one hand on her stomach. He popped the match alight and lit his cigarette. He rolled over and lay on his back and looked at the brown rings of water stains on the ceiling tiles and the way the wallpaper curled in at the edges, making the corners of the room appear to bulge, as though they were creases in flesh. A fly buzzed and tapped on the lampshade, lifting off, circling the conical shape, resting on its surface, angrily scurrying this way and that, lifting off again, pinking against the bulb, casting large, shapeless shadows on the walls. A smell of age and dampness pervaded, mixed with the coconut cream his wife used on her skin, blended to a further degree with the spicy edge of his tobacco.

He could see that she was crying.

"Are you thinking about her?" he asked. She nodded and wiped her face with the backs of her hands. "Talk to me," he said and held out his hand again. She looked at him and he began to say something else which was lost in the thunder that came and went in the sky.

"Tell me again about the thunder," she said.

"Don't you want to talk about Marie?"

"Don't call her that."

My wife's name was the name of her mother and her mother's mother. I always hated that. It smacked of laziness. I hate it now that all their names are on the gravestone – loving daughter of, loving granddaughter of. She is becoming homogenised. Her name is becoming meaningless. Its repetition is hypnotic.

"What do you want to call her?"

"I don't want to give her a name at all."

"She's *got* to have a name."

"It will make her dead."

"But she *is* dead."

If I speak her name I toss meaning onto a river that flows endlessly away. It gets smaller and smaller. *She* recedes into some past, some history that makes everything dead *dead*. Gradually her name and the reality of *her* become so utterly separated that she ceases to exist.

"I know."

"So what do I tell them?" he said.

"Cremation," she answered and filled up a tumbler from the tap.
"If that's what you want."
"But I don't want a headstone."
"Don't you *want* to remember her?"

I want to remember *her*, not a name scraped into marble. The stones of the dead help us only to forget. Burial is always about forgetting, covering, moving on, – think of the metaphors: *bury the hatchet, bury your head, bury the past.*

"Of course I want to remember her, but not like that."
"What about me? Don't I get to say anything? I *am* her father."
"And what would you do?"
"Bury her with dignity and decency, with a stone above her grave. Have her name carved out in big fucking letters. That's what I'd do."

What does a stone, a name and two dates achieve? Her life and death were separated by exactly thirty years. She died on her birthday. The dates on her grave differ by one number – a single digit communicates that a life has been and gone. It is easy to miss.

I got wet this morning because I was altering her gravestone.

I have taken a chisel to the marble and carved out parentheses, enclosing the dates, her life, with the symbols of possibility. Now her life is something more than stone. There is *before* and there is *after*. The dates are incidental; they ought not to be read with any seriousness; they are an aside within a bigger *she*.

That sounds awfully pretentious. It isn't meant to be. I was trying to say something about the way she feels larger than a single number to me, larger than rock and language, and I don't know how to explain it.

"You bury her with a name and all you'll have is a piece of stone in a field. You'll mourn a stone and not her."

"Why are you making this so difficult?"

"Because I want you to be happy. She's worth more than a few feet of marble."

"But we'll forget her if there's nothing."

"We wont forget her."

"I'll be happy if you let me bury her, properly."

"Then bury her, but I won't come."

He lit another cigarette and massaged the bridge of his nose. "I can't believe you're being like this. We lost our baby yesterday."

"And she's still lost now."

"You didn't want her anyway, did you?"

"I did. More than anything. I'm not sure you did though."

"At first I didn't, but then I did."

"Me too."

"Do you regret getting married?"

"No. It was the right thing to do."

"Even at our age?"

We married less than a year after we met. Out of love, yes, but more because the pain of being separated had worn us to exhaustion.

113

We were twenty six when we married. She asked me if I felt I was too young. I said I didn't but I did. Not that it mattered. I loved her. I felt ripped open when I was in London and she was in France. It didn't matter about things like age. It mattered that we were not alone.

I wrote dreadful, melodramatic poems about death and desire when we were apart. She said she loved them. I cannot bear to look at them now.

I felt too young at the start of our marriage; too old at the end.

Our marriage lasted three years. Three years which occurred two decades ago. Three years that are slowly becoming drowned in amongst all the other friends and lovers, arguments, affairs and words. I have tried. I have always tried to keep her afloat.

The ceiling creaked, as the residents of the room above them returned. They both looked up for a moment.

"I'm going to start packing," she said and pulled out the two suitcases from under the sink and plumped them down on the bed. The man curled up his legs to accommodate the cases and watched her moving to the wardrobe opposite, which was so enormous that the bed had to be moved in order to open the doors fully. She reached inside with her full arm and her face pressed to the veneered door and groped around for the clothes they had hung there on their first day in the city.

They began to hear a whimpering sound in the room above them.

"They're doing it again," the woman said and pulled out a handful of dresses and shirts. She stuffed them into one of the open suitcases.

"It doesn't last long," he said.

"She sounded like a dog last time."

"Shall I put on the radio?" he asked and she nodded before retrieving a pair of his trousers from the wardrobe.

He rolled over to her side of the bed and turned the switch on the wall. Lazy jazz spread across the room, the end of *Paper Moon* sung in French. Then something slower, the articulation of heavy heat, the notes from a piano hanging separately from one another, appearing and disappearing like stars above the slow hiss of brushes on drums. He turned the volume up until the speakers buzzed.

Michel would sing at the piano at those parties in the evenings of the long summertime. It would be dark and cool and he would wheel the piano onto the balcony and entertain. He warbled like Piaf and everyone laughed. I asked him to sing *Paper Moon*. He was unsure of the translation. But he sang it anyway and everyone understood.

Michel was a friend of my publisher and liked to think of himself as a nurturer of new talent. There were others at his parties: actors, poets, musicians, dancers, painters. That's where I met my wife. She was a painter. She was a painting. She seemed fluid, like a watercolour. She painted my portrait a few days after we met. It was terrible but I didn't tell her that. I took it back to London with me and missed her almost to the point of suicide.

I can't remember what I felt when I first saw her. I don't really remember that first party of Michel's at all. More vividly I remember a few days later sitting for that portrait – scrutinising every aspect of her: the dark hair, her face, the long fingers tipped with nail varnish, the paint-smeared shirt that was open to her bosom and rolled to the biceps, her bare feet covered in dust. We married exactly a year after the date she scribbled in corner of the painting.

She said nothing and continued to fill their suitcases. Finally she pulled out a jacket from the wardrobe and held it up in front of her. He had bought it from a junk shop around the corner from the hotel on the second day of their holiday in Paris.

That's when the pain had started. In the shop she felt nauseous but once outside the pain became unbearable. They rushed back to the hotel. An ambulance was called. They sat in the lobby, feeling alien suddenly to one another. They got to the hospital. The baby was delivered. It was six weeks early. It lived for three hours. And afterwards a midwife wrapped the child in a white flannel sheet and placed it in the Perspex cot next to the woman's bed.

They sat separately on the bed; she in a hospital gown spotted with blood, and he with the junk shop jacket over his knees. The woman and her husband looked at the child, which was inconceivably small; smaller than the smallness they had prepared themselves to witness. It was very white, the skin dry and flaky. Its head was turned towards them. It had a patch of long dark hairs at the front of its scalp, which the nurse cut off and gave to the woman who gave them in turn to her husband.

Then they went back to looking at the baby. Its eyes were open; they were very black. They stared at its eyes for an hour. Then it was taken away. Then they never saw it again.

Then is like a drumbeat. It regulates life. It is the name that we have given to the ticking noise inside the clock of memory, which is not calibrated in seconds and minutes or months or years, but *then*.

We had been married for more or less three years and Michel had invited us over again for the summer. On her birthday, a Sunday at the end of August, we caught a train to le Grande Jatte. A sweaty haze was giving way to the gloom of black clouds gathering over the Bois de Boulogne. We went down to the edge of the Seine and ate the food we'd brought off a blanket. When we'd finished she swam out into the river. Then she waved at me and I waved back. Then I watched her swimming back and forth under the milling shadows of oak trees. Then it began to rain. Then the thunder came. Then she began to swim back to me. Then she lost her glasses in the water. Then she dived to find them. Then she disappeared. Then.

In a sentence that only consists of *then*, the full stop erases the future.

He turned off the music. There was no noise from upstairs. Rain formed a constant hiss in the background and a spattering noise closer to them as it spilled from the broken guttering onto the balcony.

"Do you still want this?" she asked and he gestured for her to pass the jacket to him.

"I never got to try it on," he said and got up from the bed, the sheets sticking to his skin.

"You're not going to *wear* it are you? It's filthy."

"Of course, that's why I bought it."

He pulled the jacket on and jerked it at the edges to make it fit. It was too small for him. The cuffs rode up to past his wrists and the length was odd. It ought to have fallen to the upper part of the thigh but it came only to his waist.

"Who do you think this belonged to?" he asked.

"Well they were smaller than you, whoever it was," she said.

He continued to yank and smooth the jacket.

"You can't make it *grow* any more," she said and then became irritated by his constant fussing with the jacket. "Stand still, for God's sake."

He stopped.

"Can you even *move* in it?" She said and he opened his arms and the jacket lifted and parted like curtains to expose his body: the dark expanse of hair, the watery belly, the genitals squashed against his legs. "Take it off," she said. "I want to pack it."

"Hold on," he muttered and put his hand into the left pocket. His fingers came through the lining "It's gone," he said.

"What's gone?"

"The hair, the baby's hair. I put it in this pocket and it's fallen out."

He took the jacket off and laid it out on the bed, turning all the pockets inside out and picking out the hairs that were left. He held them up to the light one by one and threw them away. They were long and white. He got down on his knees and began picking at the carpet, raking it with his fingernails trying to find the baby's hair. When he could find nothing but dirt and dust he beat the mattress with his fist and then buried his face in the jacket and sobbed.

Gently the woman lifted him up by the arms, removed the jacket from the bed, put it back in the wardrobe and closed the door. He began to protest but she pressed a finger to his lips.

"Tell me again about the thunder," she said.
"I can't. I can't think," he sniffed.
"You said it didn't really rumble."
"No it doesn't."
"You said it was an illusion. A trick."
"Yes."

"You said it was part of the lightning."
"It is."
"She's not coming back."

She's not coming back. I know that. Why do I feel I must drag her back from the past?

She is, by degrees, getting further and further away. Seeing her name on the gravestone makes her even more distant, and then all things distant

The lamp on the bedside table juddered as the residents of the next room returned and opened the door against the adjoining wall. They spoke in French, sometimes clearly, sometimes muffled. A baby cried.

An argument began or continued and the crying intensified and persisted through the wall, making the woman's breasts hurt. They began to swell and grow hard. She winced and went over to the sink, removing her night-gown and pressing her hands to her chest.
"What's wrong," he asked.
"My milk's coming."

The past recedes, inevitably.

The longer I live, the further she is removed from the world. She has become a myth of my life, the art of my life, reduced to seven or eight visions, each more and more depleted and, I'm sure, inaccurate with every passing moment.

120

I will tell Michel to sell his apartment. She will become history. The woman who is a presence in my head will cease when I die and her stone will add to the public past. One more private history will end. It seems that there is a second death when you cannot be a memory anymore.

Life should be like fiction – you pick up a book and put it down, read it once, read it fifty times, the characters are always the same in the same place doing the same things at the same time, they don't change, it's an absolute. But not everyone has books written about them. I can't write one about her now. It would be full of lies. I have left it too late. I should have written down everything she said, every gesture, every shape she made with her body.

But all my novels are about her. No. No, that's not true. They are not about her; they are about *me*, the feelings that her absence stirs in *me*. I see it now. I unwind my work like a ball of string to try and find her but find only *me*, the inevitability of *me*.

She fades like an idea. Like the furthest edge of thunder.

She leant over the sink, and began to knead her breasts, clamping them between her palms and smoothing the thick colostrum out. Blue veins swelled in the things in her hands. They looked detached from her; small, pathetic animals that she was trying to save. She was swearing under her breath. The baby started to scream next door. He could not bear to watch her but could not think of anything else.

He wanted to be ignorant of all this. He felt repulsed by her, by himself, the room, the child.

They never found her. She was never washed up as many that drown in the river are. We buried an empty coffin. I carried it with her three brothers, but I could have carried it on my own. We buried a ghost. We buried air. We gave her name to emptiness.

When I look at the river now I feel nothing. It seems inconceivable that she is still there underneath the water, comical almost.

I think it is the sense of *movement* that prevents me feeling her presence. The river moves. The light moves on the water. She moves with it. It passes her along the bowbends, and the lines the river swells to follow, under bridges where the water falls to shadow for a moment, past the rows of plane trees by the roadside, past the dust and grey suburbs, outwards through a yawning flatness to the sea.

He wished that he had held the child in the hospital. He could not picture it now. Its face was unknowable. He realised that he had not touched it at all, not even stroked its cheek with his finger, not even held its hand. He thought of the word *waste* and about his wife, his strange strange wife and her milk spiralling down the ancient pipes of the hotel into the sewers; then thrust along by the torrent of rainwater; then emptied into the Seine, the dark river at the end of the street. Then.